ChangelingPress.com

Shadow/Carnage Duet
A Bones MC Romance
Marteeka Karland

Shadow/Carnage Duet
A Bones MC Romance
Marteeka Karland

All rights reserved.
Copyright ©2023 Marteeka Karland

ISBN: 978-1-60521-859-5

Publisher:
Changeling Press LLC
315 N. Centre St.
Martinsburg, WV 25404
ChangelingPress.com

Printed in the U.S.A.

Editor: Katriena Knights
Cover Artist: Marteeka Karland

The individual stories in this anthology have been previously released in E-Book format.

No part of this publication may be reproduced or shared by any electronic or mechanical means, including but not limited to reprinting, photocopying, or digital reproduction, without prior written permission from Changeling Press LLC.

This book contains sexually explicit scenes and adult language which some may find offensive and which is not appropriate for a young audience. Changeling Press books are for sale to adults, only, as defined by the laws of the country in which you made your purchase.

Table of Contents

Shadow (Bones MC 10) 4
   Chapter One 5
   Chapter Two 24
   Chapter Three 38
   Chapter Four 53
   Chapter Five 64
   Chapter Six 79
   Chapter Seven 94
   Chapter Eight 111
Carnage Bones (MC 11) 123
   Chapter One 124
   Chapter Two 136
   Chapter Three 156
   Chapter Four 175
   Chapter Five 194
   Chapter Six 206
   Chapter Seven 220
Marteeka Karland 234
Changeling Press E-Books 235

Shadow (Bones MC 10)
A Bones MC Romance
Marteeka Karland

Millie: Venus and I have always clashed. Now she's hell bent on rescuing our little sister, Katya. Which I agree with. Except I tried to get the bitch to go after Katya when we escaped, four years ago. Before I can kill Venus I get a look at the man standing behind her. *Shadow*. Talk, dark, and dangerous doesn't begin to cover him. He's hella big, with a wicked sense of humor that never seems to waver, no matter how much I insult him. He's all that keeps Venus and me from tearing each other apart. And I want him. Oh, I pretend it's just a fling, but Shadow has other plans. He's also got some anger management issues we need to deal with. That's OK, though. I have some issues of my own.

Shadow: I'm the rock of my club. The mild mannered one with a quick wit. But there's a reason they call me Shadow, and it's not the color of my skin or the way I blend into the night, so no one can see death coming. There's a darkness in my soul. A rage that sometimes burns out of control. But then I meet my little Millie. She's fierce in a tiny package. Can probably even take me in a fight. And I want her desperately.

Chapter One

"They call her *The Russian*," Venus said as they walked into the underground garage where fights had been set up for the night. "Is different from fight Samson fought with Fury couple years back. This one's fight-until-you-lose kind of thing."

Word was there was a fighter who hadn't been beaten since she'd started. Venus was convinced this woman was her sister. "Have you seen her fight?" Shadow asked.

"*Nyet*. But Data said his wife, Zora, made positive ID through Russian hacker friend." Venus shrugged. "I'll know soon."

Shadow just grinned and shook his head, following Venus into the fray. It wasn't like the woman was inconspicuous or anything. She dressed from head to toe in hot pink. Her hair and nails and lips were pink, as well as her bike. Her fucking *eyes* were pink. That and her accent, and she stood out something fierce. Shadow didn't mind, though. Made it easier for him to blend in. He was fucking big but disappearing in a crowd or in the shadows was his specialty. It was how he'd gotten his road name. Not because he was a very dark-skinned African American. Because he could just vanish when he wanted to. Right in plain sight. Having such a flamboyant traveling companion made it that much easier.

The crowd let up a roar in celebration as the announcer called the end of the match. There were angry shouts but not the killing rage like he'd experienced when Fury's ol' lady had kicked Shadow's ass. He smiled remembering that night. Yeah, they'd almost died, but Shadow could just imagine the shocked silence that followed him hitting the mat like a big fucking tree being felled.

As they approached the ring, Shadow scanned the place, looking for the girl in question. He had no idea who he was looking for, but he figured he'd know her when he saw her. *The Russian*. Right.

"Look," Venus said, her voice barely above a whisper. Had he not been so close to her, Shadow wasn't sure he'd have heard her. "There she is." The woman looked proud as a motherfucker. Her smile was carnivorously, *viciously* gleeful. Shadow couldn't blame her. "My little sister, Lyudmila."

"Handful of a name," Shadow commented as he sized the girl up.

"Handful of a girl." Venus grinned. "Always was. I called her Millie just to piss her off, but it stuck."

The man they carried out of the ring wasn't as big as Shadow, but he was just as muscular. That wasn't the issue, though. The woman who'd fought him stood in the corner of the ring, braced on one hand against the turnbuckle, her hip cocked. She had short-cropped hair dyed in several shades of blue from a pale turquoise to nearly black. In her other hand, she had a joint she pulled from occasionally while they cleaned up the mess behind her. And she *might* have been five feet tall. Maybe. If she were in heels.

Shadow felt his face split into a big grin. "Wee little thing."

"Don't let size fool you. She packs punch." Venus couldn't have sounded more proud.

The little thing wore a black vest and black pants. Both looked to be leather. Both were studded with silver spikes at the seams and around her waist. Matching black wristbands accompanied the vest and pants, as well as a studded dog collar. She wore dark makeup over her pale skin so that around her eyes was blackened, and her cheeks were highlighted in a very dark blue that matched her lipstick. Rounding up the outfit were thick black boots. All in all, very Goth.

With that outfit, Shadow expected loads of piercings and tats but saw none. Not even a piercing in her delicate earlobes. The closer he got, the more she appealed to him. He couldn't help but grin. "I think I'm in love with your sister, Venus. Just throwing that out there."

Venus chuckled, but there was no humor in the sound. "Good luck with that."

The announcer laid out the next round, though Shadow wasn't paying much attention. He was sizing up the young woman in front of him. She was younger than Venus but seemed harder. Like she'd love nothing more than to take a motherfucker out just because she'd had a bad morning.

Her opponent ducked into the ring, and they closed the cage door, locking them both in. The man she was supposed to fight this time was smaller. Leaner and shorter, but he held himself like he knew what he was doing. He didn't waste time showboating or playing up the crowd. He just assumed a boxer's stance and danced from foot to foot waiting on the call to battle. Millie just stood there, her back to him, calmly taking another hit from her joint.

The instant the bell rang, the man charged. Millie whirled around just as he bore down on her, shoving the lit end of her joint in his eye. The man screamed in agony, covering his eye with both hands and shuffling backward so abruptly that he fell on his ass. Millie pounced, straddling his chest, pinning his arms with her knees as she proceeded to pound the now defenseless man into the mat. Blood sprayed where her fists connected with his nose. The man didn't offer any defense after the first three or four blows, and the ref finally pulled Millie off him. She calmly walked back to her corner to stand, again facing away from the center.

The crowd roared its approval. Shadow just grinned. "Yeah, I'm totally in love."

"You realize she's not like Fury's woman, *da*? She could kick your ass anytime she wants."

"Yeah," Shadow said, only half paying attention. His focus was entirely on the small woman in the corner. As men helped the other fighter to his feet, he finally got his bearings and shrugged the men off him. With a rage-filled battle cry, he charged Millie once again.

At first, she didn't move. Then, at the very last instant, she turned, driving the heel of her hand with the force of her body weight straight into the guy's throat. The force of her strike, combined with the guy's forward momentum, was too much for his fragile neck. He dropped to the ground writhing and clutching at his throat, gasping for breath. This time, since he'd refused to leave the ring the first time, everyone just waited to see what would happen. The crowd grew quiet while the fighter's last death rattles finished. He finally stilled, his hands at his neck, eyes wide in disbelief as his face went slack in death. Then the crowd roared its approval. Yeah. Millie had just crushed her opponent's windpipe, killing him.

She'd just killed a man. Granted, the guy was coming for her back like a coward. But it really shouldn't have turned Shadow on. It did. Shadow grinned, crossing his arms over his chest. "Girl has some fight in her."

"That she does," Venus agreed.

They made their way to Millie's corner where she'd calmly turned back, facing the outside of the cage. Instead of smoking a joint, she took a long pull of vodka straight from the bottle. Shadow raised an eyebrow at Venus, who just shrugged. Finally, Millie's gaze fell to her sister. Instead of a warm greeting, Millie just scowled, spitting on the mat as she eyed her sister. Then she turned her back on them. Shadow was certain she hadn't even registered his presence. If she did, she didn't expect him to be with Venus. Which was fine with him. The longer she remained oblivious to him, the more time he had to study her.

When the announcer told them all bets were final, signaling the end of the competition, Millie headed for the cage door. Shadow expected Venus would hurry to meet her sister, but the woman just stood there, running her sharpened nails back and forth across one of the cage bars.

"Shouldn't we go to her?"

Venus shrugged. "*Nyet*. She will come to me."

Sure enough, a few minutes later, the little pixie came stomping over to her older sister. "This better be good."

"Mama is dead."

"Jesus, Venus," Shadow muttered. "Way to soften the blow."

Venus just shrugged. "Life isn't soft, you big pussy. She learned that long ago. Same as me."

Sure enough, Millie just looked from Venus to Shadow and back. Shadow got the sense she'd dismissed him the second she saw him. Which kind of made him want to grunt and flex his muscles at her. Show her he was not, indeed, a pussy.

"Who's the big pussy?" Millie asked, quirking an eyebrow. Shadow had to fight a grin and do his best to scowl. He really liked this girl. She might not grin at him now, but he'd just bet she was having a ball at his expense.

"Just some guy who thinks women need protection." Venus rolled her eyes at him. "We need to talk."

Millie just glared at Venus. In all the time he'd been around Venus since he came to Salvation's Bane, he'd never seen anyone -- man or woman -- look at the woman the way her sister did. No one would dare. Even the men gave her a wide berth sometimes.

"Meet me at docks in an hour."

"*Nyet*," Venus said immediately. "We go now."

"*Ty khochesh' vstretit'sya? Ty delayesh' eto v moye vremya. Ne vash,*" Millie said, glancing at Shadow and smirking. As if he didn't know exactly what she'd said.

"Darlin'," he drawled. "There's a nine-year-old little girl out there who says we can't do this on your time. You can be part of the solution or not, but we leave for Belarus in an hour. So yeah. We doin' this on our time."

Millie gave him another look, this one a little more involved. She didn't dismiss him out of hand like before. Without taking her clear blue gaze from his, she asked Venus, "Who did you say pussy is?"

"Name's Shadow," he said before Venus could answer. "I work with your sister."

"He also is adept at eavesdropping. Heard conversation I had with friend in FSB. My friend said our mother is dead and her husband is looking to get rid of Katya. He didn't know why, only that time was of the essence."

"*Blyad*!" Millie looked like she wanted to punch something, but settled for staring at Venus with a hard glare. "You're sure? You're absolutely sure? Did he go back to Russia?"

"*Nyet*. He stayed in Belarus where he's most

comfortable." Venus was obviously confident her information was correct. She spoke immediately and concisely. "I wouldn't be here if I wasn't sure."

Millie looked at Shadow again. "You speak Russian." It wasn't a question. When he nodded, she shrugged. "Perhaps you will be more useful than you look."

"Yeah," Shadow said with a grin. "The big dumb brute has more than two brain cells to rub together."

Millie *tsked*. "So touchy. Don't you have friends who aren't pussies, Venus?"

Venus just shrugged. "He has his uses. Brawn is a wonderful thing to have sometimes."

"If we leave in an hour, I assume you already have travel planned?"

"We do. Jet's waitin' on the tarmac," Shadow said. "Venus said we'd need you, but if you ain't goin'…"

Millie gave him an impatient look before turning to speak to Venus. "If we're going to Belarus, I have something I need to retrieve. Give me location, and I meet you in thirty minutes."

Venus shook her head. "*Nyet*, little sister. You come with us now, or not at all." Venus's face was hard. When she spoke of her younger sister, it had always been with a soft smile that Shadow had a hard time reconciling with the hard woman he knew Venus to be. "This comes directly from my boss. No one must know we left country, and I will not take chance on you contacting your lover in palace. Tipping him off. We need you to get Katya, but I don't trust you."

"Ouch," Millie said with a mock wince. "You sure know how to hit girl where it hurts."

"Considering you nearly got us killed last time, you'll understand why I won't take chances."

"Fuck you, Ulyana! You have no idea what really happened! You don't want my help? Fine! See how far you get without me. *Blyad*! I don't even know why you came for me in first place! But I promise, you'll get little Katya killed without me."

Venus raised an eyebrow. "What do you know that I don't?"

"What?" Millie gave her a wide-eyed look of complete innocence. "Did you think Victor wouldn't keep tabs on little Katya? You leave with her, she dies."

"You're gonna have to explain this one," Shadow said, losing patience with the whole affair. "But we ain't got time to wait." Instead of arguing with the two women, he grabbed both of them by the arm and urged them in the direction of the exit. They needed to get out of here and on the road. They had a small window to slip out of U.S. air space without being noticed. And he had the feeling they needed not to be noticed.

"What the fuck?" Millie spat at him, struggling. Shadow knew if she wanted to get free, it would be an easy thing for her, but he was betting she'd rather go with them than risk being left behind.

"We're on a bit of a tight schedule, ma'am," he said as he kept moving them until they reached his and Venus's bikes.

"Pink, Ulyana? Really? You must have a pussy for a president if he lets you keep that at his clubhouse."

Without warning, Venus struck out, slapping Millie full on the face. Instead of retaliating, Millie just looked at Venus like a naughty child who'd overplayed her hand, in complete and utter shock.

"We don't have time for this, *rebenok*. We need to get to plane and get airborne. Now."

Shadow raised an eyebrow but said nothing. He didn't have a helmet on his bike, but he figured Millie wouldn't wear one anyway. On the way here, he'd thought Millie would ride with Venus. Appeared that wouldn't be the case.

"Come on, wildcat," he murmured to her. "Climb on behind me."

* * *

Lyudmila climbed on the back of the big Harley behind Shadow. If she'd ever met a larger man she couldn't remember when. He wore dark jeans and a dark T-shirt, his muscles stretching the material almost to bursting. Kinda reminded her of the Hulk. And, God, a man with that much muscle turned her the fuck on!

The name Shadow suited him in more ways than one. His skin was black as night, his eyes just as dark. Even with his size, Millie had nearly missed him at first. Her sister was flamboyant, sticking out like a target in that ridiculous pink getup she had going on, but it effectively kept the attention on her, rather than her companion. Shadow took advantage of that diversion. She admired and respected his abilities. The fact that he understood Russian was a surprise as well. Apparently he had brains as well as brawn.

Then there was her sister. Ulyana. Venus she went by now. Her club name. As if she could outrun the past by drowning herself in pink and changing her name to the goddess of fucking love. They were killers. Both of them. She wasn't certain Ulyana actually tried to hide what she was, but she certainly downplayed it. Millie, on the other hand, embraced it. She'd been trained to kill from the time she started school. What she never expected was to be on the back of a man's bike flying down the road to a plane headed back to

Belarus. The only thing there besides her niece was death. Death and sorrow.

They pulled into the private airport. The jet wasn't more than a small cargo jet. The exterior was a light gray with a yellow-and-red stripe while the inside was a big empty hull. Shadow drove his bike straight inside, followed by Venus. Both shut their machines off, then proceed to lash them down.

"We depart in ten minutes," a big man yelled from the front. "You're both under orders not to get killed."

"Yeah?" Shadow said. "That's one order we both intend on followin'."

Venus said nothing, just secured her bike, then went to the black crates that were already loaded. "Looks like Cain armed you well."

Shadow grinned at Venus. "I told you he'd come through for us."

Millie watched the interaction, hoping they'd leave her be for a while. Her face still stung where her sister had slapped her. There might have been a couple of small scratches where those wicked nails of hers had dug into Millie's cheek.

"There should be any weapon we need, and some computer equipment, though, I'll admit, I'm not the best at that kinda shit. We'll have to find little Katya the old-fashioned way."

"*Nyet*," Venus said, looking straight at Millie. "That's why I insisted on finding her."

Shadow glanced at her, then back to Venus. "How's she helpin'?"

"She knows layout and, apparently, something regarding how they keep track of Katya."

Shadow raised an eyebrow at her. "Well? You gonna spill it?"

"It's complicated," Millie said with a shrug.

"Well, we got about twelve hours. Surely in that time you can help us pussies understand whatever it is we need to know." There was a look of amusement on Shadow's face, but she got the feeling it was as much a reprimand as anything else.

"Everyone in their seats," a voice from the overhead speaker commanded. "We're taking off."

Shadow grabbed Millie's arm and dragged her to some seats lining the front bulkhead facing the back of the plane. "Fasten your seat belt," he commanded as he sat and did the same. Venus sat on the other side of him and fastened her own seat belt.

Millie was a fighter. A killer. She'd routinely stared death in the face and smiled. But she was fucking *terrified* of flying. Gripping the edges of the seat as the plane started to move, Millie closed her eyes tight, sweat starting to bead her upper lip and forehead and drip into her eyes. They must be taxiing down the runway to get in position to take off. Her breath came in shallow gasps. Then the plane turned before stopping. The engines began a steady acceleration, whining as the pilot prepared for takeoff.

She must have let out a whimper because Shadow patted her arm. "Don't worry. Deke can fly anything with wings." He grinned. "Ain't bad with the landin' either." He had a soft, Southern drawl that Millie was sure could melt panties all over Florida. Hell, she'd drop hers if she weren't in the beginnings of a panic attack.

"*Blyad*," she swore softly. "*Eto pizdets*."

"Ain't nothin fucked up about it, sugar. Just a plane."

"She doesn't like flying," Venus supplied, looking rather bored. She smirked at Millie. "Now who's pussy?" Yeah. Millie deserved that.

"*Suka.*"

Venus just snorted before turning away. She didn't like flying any more than Millie did. Their mad dash out of Belarus four years earlier had seen to that.

"What did you mean when you said Victor would keep tabs on Katya?" Shadow spoke, but Millie barely registered his words. "Millie? Come on, honey. You gotta breathe."

"*Blyad… Blyad!*" She chanted the word over and over. Sweat dripped steadily down her face, and she shivered uncontrollably. A quick glance at her sister told her she wasn't in much better shape, but Venus held herself together much better than Millie. Still, her jaw was clenched and her eyes tightly closed.

"You gals got some serious issues with flying, huh?" Shadow muttered. "Here, Millie. Hold my hand." He pried the fingers of her right hand loose and took it in his big one. He laced their fingers together, and Millie clung to him. "Easy, sugar," he said, wincing a little. She tried to look at him, but her vision wouldn't focus. Besides, moving her head meant chancing a glance out one of the few windows where everything was starting to whizz by. The plane was taking off, streaking down the runway at a million miles an hour, plastering her against her shoulder harness since the seats faced the rear of the plane. It took all Millie had to bite her lip and keep from crying out. Or worse, being sick. When she didn't let up on his hand -- she honestly couldn't -- Shadow said nothing, just held her clenched hand in his bigger one.

It was several minutes before the machine leveled out and the ride became smoother. The immediate terror passed. Millie still gasped for breath. Shadow undid his harness, then knelt in front of her.

"Look at me, sugar," he said. That soft, deep voice commanded her attention. "Come on. Eyes up."

Somehow, Millie managed. He gave her a gentle smile. "There's my girl. Let me see your pretty blue eyes." She took a deep breath, closing her eyes briefly before opening them again to an even bigger smile. "Yeah," he said with a satisfied nod. "You're back with me. Good. I'll get you a bottle of water. Be right back."

That was it. No condemnation. No making fun of her. Just… whatever that was. It wasn't long before he was back with a cold bottle of water. He handed one to Venus, then knelt in front of Millie again, watching while she took a healthy pull.

"You good?" Shadow met her gaze steadily. She sighed, wiping a shaking hand over her face.

"Fine."

He raised an eyebrow at that, but let it go. Shadow stood and went to Venus. "We've got just over eleven hours to plan this. You ready?"

"*Da*," she said, standing and retrieving a laptop from an overhead bin. "Millie, I need to know what you know. If we're to do this right, you have to tell us everything."

This was the most embarrassing situation she'd ever been in. She'd nearly had a fucking panic attack in front of a stranger. A stranger she had to work with, who already judged her on her size and not her capabilities. It made her want to punch something. Preferably her fucking sister.

She shot Venus a look. "If you'd bothered to see beyond relationship I was pretending to build with Mikhail, maybe you'd know same shit I do. Which, I'd like to point out, cost him his position in palace when you berated me for fucking a common soldier. I wasn't fucking him. He was trying to help get all of us out of

Belarus together. Besides, had he still been in fucking palace, I'd have known Katya was in danger and could have gotten her out before whatever contact in fuckin' FSB informed you! So fuck you!"

Venus didn't rise to the bait, simply looked at Millie. She'd always thought herself superior to her little sister. When she'd been a scared teenager, knowing she'd eventually have to leave, she'd followed Venus willingly because the other woman was a trained FSB member. Once they got to America, months later, Millie had been on a constant crash course on how to take care of herself and had realized that all Venus's training hadn't prepared her for the real world any more than Millie had been. They both had had to learn street sense, but Venus had never admitted to not knowing everything. Likely the doctrine of her training. If she'd doubted herself, she'd make more costly mistakes than being wrong. As part of an armed unit that was all well and good. As two women alone on the streets in various foreign countries? Not so much. Studying Venus, Millie knew she'd hit a nerve. The slight tic in her sister's right eye was a clear indication. Yeah. She wanted this fight.

To Millie's everlasting irritation, Shadow just had to step in instead of letting Millie stir some more in the hornet's nest. "We need to know what you know, Millie," he said gently. "You're probably right, but the past is done. We have to deal with the here and now."

If the man hadn't been so fucking patient and single-minded she might have found him attractive. He was certainly worthy of some masturbation material when she was alone, but the mere fact he didn't recognize she needed this fight with her sister took him out of the running for mutual gratification later. Well, that *and* he was in her sister's MC. She'd never cross that line. Not out of respect for Venus. Quite the opposite. If they put up with her sister, she had no time for them. All that aside, she knew she needed to tell them what they were up against. Because Millie knew there was no way she could do this without all the resources these two had available.

She sighed, blowing a stray lock of hair out of her eyes. "Fine. Victor has her microchipped. Like fucking dog. Mikhail says he knows of two chips in her. Second one is safeguard in case first fails. He says tech guy told Victor they would last a minimum of twenty years, but Victor insisted she have two."

"Do you know where on her body they are?"

"One is in her back at her hip. I'm not sure which side. Second, I have no idea. You'll need to find scanner he uses or chips' frequency to find either without simply cutting her open."

"*Blyad*," Venus swore, turning away and pacing several feet before focusing on her laptop.

"It's not that bad," Shadow said, hooking a finger over his chin and rubbing as he thought. "Cain can talk to Giovanni about it. I'm sure he can come up with a solution in eleven hours."

"Who's Giovanni?"

"Giovanni Romano. From Argent Tech."

Millie raised her eyebrows. "That's serious tech guy. But kind of out there for MC to be asking favors."

Shadow grinned. "Yeah. We ain't no ordinary MCs, babe. And our friends are more than a little connected."

Millie scowled. "I'm not your babe. You wanted my help? Here I am. But don't make mistake of thinking I'm your friend. Once we have Katya safely out of Victor's reach, I'm gone."

"Yeah?" Shadow raised his eyebrows. "Keep

your options open. We might have a place for you either at Bones or Salvation's Bane. Hell, Cain might offer you a position in ExFil. Most of the patched members work for him."

"Who says I'm interested? I've heard of ExFil. Word has it they are best of best. Elite soldiers. I work alone. Not with team."

"Yet, here you are." The infuriating bastard had the audacity to chuckle. "You do realize we'll be doing this as a team. Right?"

She stood abruptly. Instead of standing with her, as most men would have, he just continued to squat in front of her. The bastard was nearly as tall squatting as she was standing up. He just looked up at her in amusement. Which infuriated her.

"There's something wrong with you," she muttered. "Big bastard." Then she turned and marched over to her bag. "I need to wash blood and sweat off. Change clothes. Where's fucking bathroom?"

Shadow pointed to a narrow door. "It ain't too big. You're just a little thing. You can probably close the door when you're inside. Might still need to back in. There's a sink, though."

"*Blyad*," she swore. "Can you not do anything easy way, Ulyana? I mean, is it too much to ask to shit in private?"

"I didn't choose plane," Venus said with a dismissive wave of her hand as she continued to study her laptop screen. "Quit whining and do your business. Or you can hold it until we land."

Millie grabbed a towel from her bag and stomped off to the bathroom. It was, indeed, just as tiny as Shadow had predicted. And, no, she couldn't shut the door and sit on the toilet without spreading her knees wide. The door opened outward but left no room for anything other than the toilet.

Leaving the door open, she stripped down to her underwear and sports bra. The water was cold -- no hot water, naturally -- but at least there was some. With hurried movements, she washed the sweat and blood off her body. Her hands were a little beat up, but nothing a little acetaminophen and ibuprofen wouldn't help. She rinsed the towel before going back to her bag.

Millie wasn't a prude or anything, but she didn't generally go around changing clothes to the skin in public. In this case, though, she didn't have a choice. If Shadow got offended, fuck him.

She glanced behind her once before stripping off her bra and wiping her breasts with the wet towel, then donned a clean bra before doing the same with her underwear. She gave herself a cursory wash front and back before slipping into more boxer briefs. Not sexy, but she wasn't trying to impress anyone, and they were decidedly more comfortable than a fucking thong.

"I coulda found you a more private place if you'd just given me a minute." Shadow was standing behind her. Millie whipped her head around to find him a couple feet away, his arms crossed over his wide, muscular chest. The T-shirt he wore looked like it was a couple sizes too small, but he was so big, she wondered if they even made shirts closer to his size. His forearms and biceps bulged with every movement of his arms, and she could only imagine what that freakishly large chest looked like, to say nothing of his abdomen. Hell, he probably had a fucking eight-pack. A quick glance showed that, yes, he was hard.

She scowled at him. "Not here for your viewing pleasure." Though, yeah. It gave her a thrill that a man as powerful and strong and good-looking at Shadow found her attractive. Then again, it was her and Venus on this plane with him. He had very little to choose from. Given that he and Venus were at least affiliated with the same club, he probably considered her off-limits. Which made Millie his only choice.

"Fully aware of that. Which is why I'd intended on hanging a tarp for you. There's hooks to secure cargo on the walls, so it would have been an easy thing." He shrugged. "You got in a hurry and started before I found a tarp." He grinned. "But the view was very pleasurable." So was the deep rumble voice of his. Not that she was going to point that out.

"Well, say something next time," she snapped.

"Not if it gets me views like that. You have a beautiful body, Millie. Ain't gonna pretend you don't, or that I wasn't lookin'."

Millie shrugged. "As long as you don't touch, we're good."

That must have been the exact wrong thing to say because Shadow shut down. Admittedly, she hadn't known him long, but he seemed like the type to try to smooth things over. The mediator. He was always smiling and hadn't taken offense to any barbs thrown his way by either Millie or Venus. Now, he looked hard. A man who'd been pushed past his limit and was walking away from a situation rather than confront it and possibly lose his temper. Millie found she didn't like that at all.

"Never touched a woman without her permission," he snapped. "Ain't startin' with you." Then he turned and marched to the overhead bin and snagged his own laptop. Moving to the far end of the plane, he sat and started working. Millie hadn't meant to imply she thought he'd assault her. Of all the men she'd ever met, Shadow seemed like the least likely to hurt a woman like that. Or for any reason, though she had no doubt he'd do what he had to in combat.

Fuck. She didn't have time for this. She needed to know where Katya was being kept and the layout of the place. That was her part. She could do that. And keep Katya calm if needed. She could not pull something out of her ass to find and remove the trackers. So, she really hoped Shadow was working on that instead of licking whatever wounds she'd given him. Because if she'd hurt him that much with a flippant remark, then she was a bigger asshole than even she thought.

Chapter Two

Of all the fucking things for that girl to say to him, implying he might touch her without permission was the one thing that could set him off. He'd been accused of that once. Not in a sexual way as she'd implied, but physically. The woman Shadow'd been with back then had fought verbally. She'd accused him of getting physically abusive with her. The cops had taken one look at the tearful white woman without a mark on her and the huge tattooed, muscled Black man and assumed she'd been right. Shadow had fought it, but the police had made up their minds, and the reports had made it look pretty damning for him. Thankfully, they'd settled the dispute out of court, and the charges against him had been dropped, but it had changed the course of his life.

He put all that out of his mind. Just something to think about before he got caught up in Lyudmila. She was a pistol, he'd give her that. She'd mopped up the ring with everyone they put her against. Mainly because she didn't fight by the rules. She used every dirty trick in the book, taking down men more than twice her size. Shadow liked that. It made him smile even in his dark mood. Didn't mean he'd make the mistake of seeing her as anything but the lethal, scrappy fighter he'd already seen. Because if he let himself think about her as the woman he'd glimpsed when she'd bared her body to wash and change clothes, he was fucked.

Her body had been battle-scarred and honed in the fires of war. But there were still luscious, feminine curves to be savored. Her skin was milky white, if bruised in a few places after her fights. He'd had the insane urge to wrap his body around hers protectively when he knew she wouldn't appreciate it.

Which brought him back to reality. No. A woman that fierce wouldn't want a man to protect her. She could do that on her own. And if he wrapped his naked body around hers, she'd just kick his ass for sexually assaulting her. Shadow didn't know if it was a greater crime to beat a woman or try to rape her. But he was under no illusion that Millie couldn't fight him off if he tried, even if he was hell-bent on hurting her. She might be tiny, but she was even fiercer than Venus, and the Salvation's Bane enforcer considered Venus the most dangerous member of that MC.

"Hey." Millie came up behind him. She placed a tentative hand on his shoulder. Shadow looked up from his computer and looked back at her. "I'm sorry," she said. "I didn't mean to imply you'd try to force yourself on me. I didn't mean it like it sounded."

He nodded once. "Apology accepted." He thought that would be the end of it. She didn't seem to like him.

"Will you tell me what you're working on?" She pointed to his laptop.

Shadow raised an eyebrow. "Just informing Cain what you told us and requesting an assist from the Shadow Demons."

"Who are they?"

"An organization Romano belongs to. He and two of his associates are vigilantes of a sort in Rockwell, Illinois."

"Vigilantes?"

"Yeah. They do a lot of good in the area. Keep the riffraff to a minimum in their city. At least, they're working on cleaning it up. Still several gangs underground and slums on the outskirts that need serious attention, but they're working on it."

Millie snorted. "Rich?"

"Oh, yeah. Loaded."

"Trying to make themselves feel good."

Shadow frowned at that. "Maybe. But I always got the sense they really wanted to help. Especially since Alex's woman came from the streets. She makes sure money goes where it needs to. As to the policing of the streets? I have no idea how they do it. They were just starting to intensify that part when I first met them." He shrugged. "We don't get up that way too much."

The plane shuddered. Millie stiffened, her hand going to his shoulder to steady herself. Her fingers dug into his skin almost painfully. The color drained from her face, and she sat next to him and fastened her seat belt quickly.

"We just took off an hour ago. What could possibly be wrong?"

"Relax, sugar," he said, trying to soothe her when just minutes before he'd been irritated. Maybe not at her so much as himself for crowding her and even implying sexual innuendo. "It's just turbulence."

"That's what they said last time, too. Plane crashed."

"Well, if it makes you feel better, this is a cargo plane." He pointed to the bulkhead on the far side. "Parachutes. The back of the plane opens. If it looks like we're gonna crash, we'll just put on the parachutes, open up, and jump."

"*Blyad!*"

Shadow couldn't help it. He chuckled. "You're so fearless. I never thought you'd need sedation on a plane ride."

She actually hissed at him. Like a little cat. "I do not need sedation! I just hate flying!'

"Hey." He raised his hands. "I meant no offense. You just seem a little… tense."

"When we hopped plane out of Belarus, Victor had us shot down. All the while, the pilot kept telling us everything would be fine. I have no idea how we survived, but I'm not anxious to repeat experience."

"Understandable. How'd the pilot fare?"

She snorted. "He died. Firefight few hours later. Besides, seems you've had your own bad experience. Why'd you automatically assume I thought you'd try to rape me?"

Fuck. "It's a long story. Not sure we have time for trivial things like personal issues when we need to plan this." It was a deflection, and he could tell she knew it, too, but she let it go. "Cain has Data, our intel guy, pulling the blueprints of the place they're holding Katya. Once we have that, we'll need to focus on making a plan."

"I know building." Millie shrugged. "I'll get in and get her. You guys kill that scum, Victor. We leave. Easy."

"She's always been like that," Venus supplied from her seat on the other side of the plane. "Her idea of planning to do it as she's running straight into fray." She shrugged. "A fly-by-seat-of-pants kind of gal."

"*Da*," Millie agreed, but she looked angry. "But I get results. Better than spending half day planning only to bail at end because you broke nail."

"I did *not* break nail!" Venus snapped. "Backup got delayed. If we'd gone back in for Katya and our mother without help, we'd both be dead!"

"You don't know that," Millie bit back. "Because you wouldn't even try!"

"All right, that's enough." Shadow raised his voice just enough to get the women's attention, glancing at both of them. "No use crying over spilt milk. It's over. Only thing we can do now is try to get the girl out."

"It's way more difficult now than before," Millie said. "If we can't disable trackers in her body, we fail. We fail, she dies."

"You don't know that." Venus wasn't giving up. "We could get her to U.S., and Giovanni could get trackers out then."

"Not if they kill us all first. Mikhail suspected at least one tracker was explosive. I can't confirm it is, but I can't confirm it's safe either."

Venus stared at her a long time. "You're making this up. Why? I have no idea. *Suka*!"

Instead of lashing out or attacking Venus, Millie just smiled. "Take that chance if you want. *Suka*. But she's my sister, too. And I raised her more than Mama before we left. I won't let you take chances with her life to save your own ass yet again."

To Shadow's surprise, it was Venus who launched herself at Millie. The smaller woman barely got her seat belt off before Venus was on her. Millie ducked under and backed away to give herself time to make a stand. When Venus charged again, Millie was ready.

She sidestepped the larger woman and hiked a knee into her middle. Venus winced but kept moving. Venus kept pushing, trying to get closer to Millie. Both landed a few blows, but nothing significant. Until Millie tripped her up. Venus stumbled, and Millie was on her.

With a war bellow, she tackled Venus to the ground. Venus kept fighting, but Millie, even though she was smaller than her sister, knew how to avoid punches and wasn't afraid to fight dirty. It wasn't long before blood started to fly.

Much as he enjoyed a good cat fight, this was getting serious, and Shadow had to work with these women to get the girl out. If they couldn't remain civil, he'd have to figure this out on his own.

Deciding it was time to take charge, he grabbed Millie by the waist and hauled her off Venus. "All right, that's enough!" He raised his voice. Something he rarely did. His size ensured he never had to. "Venus, one side of the plane. Millie, go to the other."

"I'm not some naughty child to send to corner," Millie spat. "She fucking started it!"

"You're a spoiled little brat!" Venus hissed at her sister. "Always were. If it wasn't Mama spoiling you, it was Papa. When Papa died, you whined constantly because you couldn't get your way. It never occurred to you Mama didn't have money to spoil you how Papa did."

"I was eight!" Millie yelled back at Venus. "I wasn't upset about things I didn't have! I was upset I didn't have my papa!"

"I said that's enough!" This time Shadow let them know he wasn't fucking around. His yelled response had both women jumping, their gazes fixed on him. "We have enough shit to worry about without you two at each other's throats."

Just as he finished speaking, his computer gave off a little *ding*. Incoming mail. With one more stern look at the women, he went to the laptop and glanced down at it. "Looks like Giovanni has something for us."

He ignored them as he downloaded the file sent by the Shadow Demons. Opening it, he found it was the layout of a house. There was a green dot on one area in what looked to be a massive room near the center of the enormous structure. The accompanying letter had instructions on how to turn his phone into something that could detect and deactivate any trackers in the girl. He also had instructions on how to get them out, assuming they were in the subcutaneous tissue and not in her muscle or deeper. Shadow had medic training in the service, but didn't really relish the thought of digging into the girl when she didn't already have an open wound. He'd also need medical supplies he probably didn't have on this plane.

"Come take a look at this, Millie," he said. "Giovanni has isolated a tracking chip he believes is your sister."

Millie glanced at the screen, then leaned in closer, her lips parting on a gasp. The she swore violently. *"Trakhni menya grubo!"* Fuck me raw. "You've got to be fuckin' kidding me!"

"Gotta tell me what's up, sugar," he said, getting a sinking feeling life was about to get complicated.

"That room they've got her in? Yeah. Not a room."

"If it's not a room, then what is it?" Shadow was rapidly losing his patience. And that was saying something for a man known for his endless patience.

Venus came over and glanced down at the map. "I know that room. Huge ballroom. I remember parties there."

"Not ballroom," Millie snapped. "At least, not *only* ballroom. He expanded it after you left for your training. It's three times as big as ballroom was. And he built a maze in it. A very complicated maze."

Venus shrugged. "So?"

"So, big guy here can't come with us. You won't fit either. I have to walk sideways. Only place it opens up is in center. Only way out is through exit. Which is most likely guarded."

"So? Go back out way you came in." Venus sounded condescending. Which was getting on Shadow's nerves as much as it was Millie's. Venus seemed to look down on her sister. Like she wasn't good enough. While Shadow had his issues with Millie, any fool could see she was more than good enough. She was highly skilled in a fight, and Shadow would be surprised if she wasn't highly intelligent.

"Sure," Millie said, throwing her hands up. "Why didn't I fucking think of that? Oh! Maybe it would be one-way door at entrance?" She scowled at Venus. "*Grebanaya suka*," she muttered.

"All right." Shadow had had enough. "If you two can't play nice in the sandbox, I'm gonna bury you both like cat turds." He looked at one, then the other. "It's your sister we're going to rescue. I'd think your time could be better spent on figuring out how to get her out of that place instead of fighting each other. You're not each other's enemy! So either work it out, or I'll tie you both up and leave you here while I get the help I need from our boys in Poland. Do you really want to be cut out of this one?"

Neither woman said anything. Millie grabbed a pen and paper and started sketching, ignoring him completely.

His phone rang. Giovanni.

"Gonna take someone with more technical knowhow to make these changes to my phone like you said."

"Don't worry about it," Giovanni said with more amusement in his voice than Shadow liked. "I've got a kid at the base who can fix it for you. I needed you to know that room the girl's being held in may not be as straightforward as it looks. I've studied her movements, and she never moves far from the center. I've managed to hack into security, and the images I'm picking up don't make a whole lot of sense. It almost looks like a... I don't know."

"A maze?" Shadow glanced at Millie. The girl was drawing out the maze on that pad she'd picked up. "Give me a bit, and I'll give you a rough layout."

"Oh, really?" Giovanni drawled.

"Yeah. One of my girls here knew why they chose that location for Katya."

"That the name of the target?"

"Yeah. Seems the maze has one entrance and one exit. The entrance has a one-way door, and the exit is likely heavily guarded."

"Makes sense from what I'm seeing. Going is slow. I don't want anyone figuring out someone has accessed their security. I'll keep you updated. In the meantime, forget about the phone. Knew it would be too much when I sent it."

"Bastard," Shadow muttered. "Give me some good news."

"Well, I've studied the device I believe we'll be working with. There are two distinct and separate pieces of hardware. One is a straightforward tracker. It gives off a signal strong enough that anyone in the house can follow it. The other is a bit more complex. If it loses signal with the house security, or with a paired handheld device, it explodes. Small detonation, but, depending on where it's implanted, potentially fatal. Definitely debilitating."

"So that has to come out. Regardless."

"Yes. Be a good idea to remove them both."

"Gonna need more equipment and drugs than I have here."

"You'll have everything you need when you land

in Poland. I've studied the tech they're using. As long as you take them out in one piece, they should continue to work uninterrupted. They aren't temperature dependent or anything like that. Kind of primitive, actually."

"Sounds pretty sophisticated to me."

Giovanni chuckled. "Not in my world, Shadow. You're going to have to take them out before you move her, though. They need to think she's where they put her. There is a possibility they can detonate the second device without losing signal if they choose to."

"Lyudmila seems to think no one can enter this maze but her, due to both my and Venus's sizes. Says she'll barely fit. And, I gotta tell ya. The girl is barely five feet and probably doesn't even weigh a hundred pounds."

"Then you better be showing her how to remove something like that. Because you absolutely cannot take those trackers out of that room. Even beyond the small perimeter she's currently confined to would be a risk. They have to stay behind."

* * *

The thoughts of going back into that maze made Millie's skin crawl. The place was positively claustrophobic. There was no way for a normal-sized, full-grown adult to get in and out. She'd had to squeeze her way through several tight spots to make it through, and that was several years ago. Right after the maze was finished. It was complicated enough she didn't think Victor would have made any changes. He'd never have thought to change it with Millie not being there to continue to practice getting through it.

And she had practiced. Every day, many times a day from the time they started building it. She'd been careful about it, but, as the security had gone up, there was no way for him to not know what she was doing. Any time anyone had asked her what she was doing, she'd grinned and said it was fun. But she knew a prison when she saw one. Since Victor had plenty of holding cells in the deepest sublevel of the palace, this cell could only be for a member of the family. She'd thought it might be her since she was never one to obey the rules. Especially after Venus had gone. But she'd managed to leave Belarus before they'd had the chance to put her there. Katya had always been timid and shy. She'd never think to find her way through the maze and memorize it. It might have even been impossible since it was built when she was still too young to explore on her own.

She'd just about finished with her rough sketch of the maze route when Shadow crouched down in front of her.

"You good?"

"Fine," she bit out. The big fucker was acting like he was better than everyone. Talking to her and Venus like they were naughty children. Sending them to opposite sides of the plane.

He sighed, shaking his head, obviously knowing that fine didn't always mean fine. "Ain't got time for this shit," he muttered to himself.

"Excuse me?" She narrowed her eyes and met his gaze. "If two of you didn't want me with you, you should have left me at fight. I don't have time for your shit either," she snapped.

"You and Venus need to work this the fuck out before we get boots on the ground. At least, if you want your Katya out alive. It's going to take everything we've got to do this, and it's off the books so we can't use anyone from ExFil in Poland. This is just the three of us. There is no help if we get caught. We're completely on our own. If I can't trust the two of you to have each other's backs --" Before he could finish, Millie interrupted him.

"You can't leave me. Not and get Katya out. You'll never fit in the maze -- not even turning sideways -- and the walls are reinforced. You can't just shove them down."

"No. But know that I'll do it myself -- without either of you -- before I take you into a place like that where I can't control the situation. It's dangerous for everyone involved and puts ExFil at risk since both Venus and I work there."

"She's my sister, Shadow." Millie was pissed, but she could understand his point. "I may have issues with her, but I will defend her to death."

"Good. Now. There are some things you and I need to go over."

"Oh, really?"

"Yes. If you're the only one able to get through the maze, then you're the one who's going to have to get the trackers out of Katya. That means I need to teach you how to incise the area and remove the foreign body, then sew her up. You'll have to do it twice, and both trackers need to be intact."

"That's going to hurt. She's just kid. Not sure that's best idea."

"It's the only idea. I'll give you some Lidocaine to numb the area you're cutting on and stitching. But we've got a limited amount of time to practice this."

"Practice?" Millie hoped she looked as incredulous as she felt. "How am I supposed to practice?"

"On me, sugar. You're going to make some incisions on my body and practice sewing them up."

"You're out of your fucking mind!"

Turns out, he wasn't. Millie not only practiced on him but Venus, too. If she slipped and cut Venus where she wasn't numb, well, it couldn't have hurt that much. It was just a small nick. Mostly. When she got to Poland, the doc who gave them the supplies had her demonstrate on him, only he'd implanted three small chips in his own body to be as realistic as possible. And Shadow and Venus thought she was crazy? She had nothing on these people.

"Fucking crazy," she muttered as she packed up the rest of the shit they thought she'd need. It had to fit tightly against her body inside her clothing, so it didn't get caught on the corners of the maze. Fuck, she hoped she hadn't gained much weight since leaving here or she was going to be in a real pickle. All in all, she had a couple of scalpels, two small bottles of numbing medicine, two needles each of three different sizes with different purposes. Two packs of sutures, and a tool to grab onto the tiny chip planted inside her sister. Giovanni had sent them pictures of something similar, so she'd have a good idea of the scale of the thing she was looking for. They'd also given her a phone with an app programmed to find the implants.

"It's another three hours to this compound," Shadow said. "We've got four hours before dark, so I suggest you both get some rest." He addressed both Millie and Venus. Millie was going on close to thirty hours without sleep so she knew she needed it, but this close to Belarus and her own personal nightmares, she knew it would be damned near impossible. And the thoughts of facing that fucking maze again… Yeah. She knew the second Shadow had shown her where in the house they were keeping Katya she'd have to go inside, but it didn't make it any easier. Sure, she hadn't told anyone how hard this was going to be. Hadn't even admitted it to herself. But now, she was feeling it. Yeah. Sleeping was probably not going to happen until she got back to the States. Who the fuck knew how long that was going to be?

Chapter Three

Shadow lay on his bunk in the large, military-style tent, arms behind his head, listening to the woman three cots over. The place slept twenty, but had been given to his team until they left. Venus had passed out within the first fifteen minutes of their claiming bunks. Woman could sleep anywhere. Her sister, on the other hand…

Millie dozed, but she never found any kind of restful sleep. She tossed and turned. And whimpered continually when she did manage to doze off. Girl had some shit going on. None of his business, but Shadow couldn't help when his protective instincts reached out to her. She was so small but had so much fire in her. Just watching her was fascinating. She was just so fucking fierce most of the time! Seeing her like this? Well. He wasn't going to be able to sit by while her past haunted her.

She moaned, then turned over, whimpering quietly. Thankfully, the rest of the guys were out doing their own thing, giving the three of them quiet and privacy while they rested up for the mission to come. Shadow glanced at his watch. They still had two-and-a-half hours. If she was going to be reliable, she had to get some real sleep. Even if it was only an hour.

With a sigh, he sat up on the bunk, then rose and walked to Millie. She was curled on her side, trembling. Sweat drenched her. Her face was wet with it, but he was also sure there were tears there. Another small whimper and Shadow couldn't stand it anymore.

"Hey, baby," he said, his voice low. "Need you to wake up for me. Can you do that?" Very carefully, he stroked her hair away from her face, pulling at the damp strands until her eyes snapped open. She sucked in a breath and turned her head so she met his gaze.

"Is it time to get up already?"

"No, sugar. You've still got a couple of hours."

There was an adorably confused look on her face, and Shadow couldn't help but smile. "Then why…"

"You're having a bad dream," he said, still stroking her hair gently.

She closed her eyes and sighed before wiping her forearm over her face. "Sorry. Did I wake you?"

"Ain't been asleep."

She stiffened. "I'll move to other side of tent."

"You'll stay right here," Shadow said, holding her gently by the shoulder when she would have risen. "Do you trust me?"

"I… what?"

"Wasn't a trick question, sugar. Do you trust me or not?"

"I suppose. You've been more than patient dealing with me and Venus. We can be handful sometimes."

He chuckled. "Yeah. You can." He lay down on the tiny cot beside her. Millie stiffened, trying to get up again, but Shadow pulled her against him, her back to his chest. She pillowed her head on his arm, and his other big arm draped loosely over her waist. "There," he rumbled next to her ear. "I'll watch over you and keep you safe. No one gets to you without going through me."

"Shadow…" she whispered.

"Shh, sugar. I've got you. Just close your eyes. You're running on adrenaline and caffeine. You need rest."

"Guess you do, too."

"Not nearly as much as you, baby. Now. You good?"

Millie nodded her head. "Yeah," she said, the word more a soft sigh. Fuck. She sounded like they'd just spent the afternoon making love and she was sated and sleepy. Shadow's arms tightened around her slightly.

"Good. Now close your eyes and sleep for me."

He didn't have to tell her twice. In fact, her breathing was already evening out, and there was a soft snore coming from her. Shadow chuckled softly, then settled in, resolving himself to ignore the hard-on he now sported.

There had only ever been one time in his life when he'd wanted to be this close to a woman, and he hadn't wanted it nearly this bad. That time had gotten him nothing but heartache and pain. Had very nearly landed him in trouble with the law. Had it not been for Stunner, a childhood friend and fellow member of Bones in Kentucky, there was a very real possibility he'd have ended up in prison instead of the military.

Millie -- Lyudmila -- however, was a world away from Carrianne. Millie was real. She said what she thought, and fuck anyone if they didn't like it. She wasn't playing some elaborate game for her own benefit. In fact, she was throwing all in to help her family. Carrianne had proven over and over she wasn't about family. Hell, even her own parents saw that now, for all the good it did. Carrianne would always be out for what was best for her. For what could get her the most money or power. Or both. Millie just wanted to live her life. If that meant she and Venus teamed up to save their sister, she'd do it, even if she and Venus didn't get along. Shadow was the same way. Whatever it took to help his brothers and sisters -- both biological and of the heart -- he'd do it. No matter the cost to him.

For thirty minutes, he held Millie. She didn't move a muscle. But she slept soundly. Her heart rate settled, and she stopped sweating. The fucking bunk was cramped as shit, but Shadow didn't mind. Hell, he'd suffer this every fucking night for the rest of his life if it meant she slept this soundly. She was hell on wheels, but there was a great vulnerability in her he doubted she even acknowledged. That vulnerability called to every protective instinct he possessed.

How had Venus not known about her nightmares? Had they not seen each other in that long a time? It kind of sounded like they might have parted ways soon after making it to the States. Sounded like Millie had been a teenager. Had she been alone all this time?

Well, that ended now. One way or another. He had no use for a woman of his own. Never again. But Cain could definitely find a place for her. Either in Bones or ExFil. Assuming her skills were what he thought they were. And more than just dirty fighting. At least, that's what he'd tell himself until he could admit otherwise.

Somewhere in there, Shadow dozed off himself. When he woke, Millie was lying on top of him, her face buried in his neck. He smiled. He'd closed his arms around her, holding her possessively. It felt better than anything he could remember. Even the one woman he'd let into his life had never felt like this. There had been his lies and her greed hanging over them then. Now, all he had was a need to protect this little warrior. Well, that, *and* he wanted to possess her.

She was beautiful in an edgy way. The blue hair. The dark makeup. The warrior capabilities. It was all crammed into this small package of sex and sin, and it made his head spin. She was so small he was afraid she'd break in his brutal embrace. But she was strong. She'd taken on men his size and won. She fought hard and dirty. Anything it took to win. But she still looked at Venus with something like hero worship. The big sister might be out of Millie's life, but the younger woman still thought she walked on water.

He glanced at his watch. Time to get up and finish preparing for the mission. Just as he nuzzled her head to wake Millie, Venus screeched angrily. The sound probably woke everyone within a mile radius.

"You little *shlyukha*!" Venus snapped. "Do you have to fuck every dick you find?"

She tried to pull Millie off by the hair, but Shadow rolled, putting himself between Millie and Venus.

"Venus, back off," Shadow bit out.

"You back off! You're just like every man out there. Can't keep dick in your pants!"

"This is none of your business, but I didn't fuck your sister." He tried to keep his voice as calm and reasonable as possible.

"Sure you did." Venus snorted. "Just like she fucked Mikhail instead of pumping him for information!"

"I got the information I needed," Millie yelled back, struggling to her feet and facing Venus. "And I didn't fuck anyone to get it. That may be how you get information, but I make allies. Not fuck buddies."

"*Suka*!"

"Sweet baby Jesus in the manger," Shadow muttered, scrubbing a hand over his face. "If the two of you can't get along, I'm only taking one of you." He stared Venus down. "Guess which one a' ya's staying here."

"Sure. Take your little *shlyukha*. See how far you

get. She'll hang you out and get you killed."

"I never knew you were such a spoiled little child, Venus," Shadow said softly. "What does it matter who your sister fucks? Why do you care so much?"

"Because Mikhail was *mine*! And she fucked him anyway!"

Millie snorted. "See, that's where you made your mistake. You let your emotions cloud your judgment. Mikhail *was* yours. *Still* would be if you hadn't accused him of fucking me. You got him fired. Probably exiled or shot! What you were too blind to see was how much he loved you." Millie tugged on her bulletproof vest, pulling it into place and fastening down the Velcro tightly. "He loved you, and you ruined his life. All because you took something you saw out of context. He leaned in, not to kiss me, but to warn me. Had we not left that night, we'd both have been sold. Just like they plan on doing with little Katya. That's why I wanted her out that night. That's why I insisted on going now even knowing there was little chance of getting out. All this?" Millie circled her finger in the air. "All this is on you. Yet, it's me risking my life to get her out. I'll be one to cut into her flesh and remove devices they put into her. You can just sit here on your ass and think of all ways I fucked you over. When this is over, I'll be gone out of your life. So fuck you. Just… fuck you."

Tears tracked down Millie's face by the time she got finished. But she sniffed once, then swiped her forearm over her eyes before spitting on the ground at Venus's feet. Then she left the tent.

Shadow stood and moved in front of Venus when she looked like she might go after Millie. "No. You stay here."

"I'm going with you."

"I think maybe it would be better if you kept an eye on things from here. Stay in command with Chase. You'll know what's going on and keep an eye on us from the command center."

"I can't believe you're cutting me out! You wouldn't even be here if it weren't for me!"

"No. I wouldn't. And you'd go in there with your sister and get all three of you killed."

"She's my sister. I can work through my emotions and keep her safe."

"Yeah? Do you know that she can? Because right now, all she knows is you just called her a whore, and that you don't have a very high opinion of her. You think she's gonna be concerned if you get the shit beat outta you?"

"Of course, she will. We're sisters."

Shadow snorted. "Yeah, well, I'm not takin' that chance. Cain made me promise to do the right thing, even if it went against what you wanted. Especially if you and Millie seemed as volatile as you appeared. He wants no mistakes, and he wants us all back in one piece with the girl."

"I'm going."

"You're staying," Shadow said firmly. "If that means I have someone tie you up and gag you, I will."

Venus looked at him like she was ready to flay the skin from his body. "If she's harmed in any way, I will fucking kill you." Her voice was soft. Deadly. But Shadow had had enough.

"You know, you could spend your time with her telling her how much you missed her, or how much you love her instead of being such a fuckin' bitch all the time, Venus." He pointed in the direction Millie had gone. "That girl worships the ground you walk on.

Anyone can see it in the way she constantly looks for your approval. On the plane, when she was terrified, she looked to you for guidance. I could tell you both had issues, but she followed your lead. Tried to keep herself under control because she didn't want to disappoint you. Maybe you should think about that." He let that sink in a moment before asking. "How long have you guys been apart?"

Venus scrubbed a hand over her face. She didn't have her usual makeup on and her face, though fiercely beautiful, looked more... real. Like her makeup was like all the fucking pink. Armor to protect her. They let people see what they wanted to see and not the dangerous, deadly woman beneath.

"She left me a few days into our escape. Right before we were to board another plane to take us to United States. We were supposed to fly to England, a little strip outside city, but we were shot down just after takeoff. Everyone but us and copilot died in crash. He died shortly afterward when Victor sent men to finish job he'd started. I was wounded, but Millie was unscathed."

"What made her leave?"

"I thought because I had all this training from FSB I knew what was best. I ignored her when she wanted to go back for Katya. Though I had wanted Katya with us all along. Our mother refused to go, and Katya was just five. Lyudmila practically raised Katya, though she was only a teenager. But if Victor decided to call it kidnapping -- which he would have -- we'd have had more than just his goons on us. After plane crash, she made one more plea. I blew her off. Then Victor's men came after us. In confusion of fight, I got her away from plane, and we stole car and got out of Belarus.

"Once in Poland, however, she tried again to make her case. Again, I refused to listen to her, thinking I was better equipped to make decisions. I'd probably have been more agreeing if Millie hadn't gone against me before we got out of palace. She tried to snag Katya on the way out. It alerted guards. We barely made it out alive. I berated her, telling her I was in charge, and I stuck to it. Deciding I'd make all the decisions from there on out. I was better educated in that area, and I was determined we'd both make it out of Belarus. Two days later, when we ran into another fight, she tried to tell me a way to avoid Victor's men altogether. I refused, and when it was all over, Millie was gone." Venus looked devastated. Like it was a personal failure on her part. And maybe it was. But hadn't they all made mistakes in their past?

"Can't beat yourself up over the past. Just learn and don't make the same errors."

"With Millie, I can't seem to help myself. We just... clash. I knew she hadn't been with Mikhail. But I saw what looked like him kissing her and I lost my mind."

"You need to find a way to make peace with her," Shadow said. "Don't miss out on your sister's love and devotion because of pride."

Venus winced, then nodded once. "I'll keep watch over you both from command center. Don't be without radio contact on hand. No matter what. I have bad feeling about this."

"Understood." Shadow had the same feeling.

He caught up with Millie as she loaded the last of their supplies into the military-issue Hummer. God, she was sexy. He had to get past that. Ignore it. Because it would spell disaster for both of them. Especially now. He didn't need to be distracted, and neither did she.

"We good to go?"

Millie glanced at him, ducking her head. "*Da.*"

"You OK?" She nodded, not saying anything or looking at him. "If it's about Venus, I'm sure she didn't mean --"

"Yes, she did. And I meant everything I said as well."

"Millie --"

"Let's go. We've got a lot to accomplish before dawn."

Right. "I'm gettin' too old for this shit," Shadow muttered. "Fine. But I'm driving."

She sneered. "Don't trust me?"

"Trust you completely. But this vehicle cost more than I could make in several years. It's on loan from my boss. So, I drive." Surprisingly, Millie only snorted before going to the passenger's side and sliding in without another word.

* * *

They made the ride to their staging area in silence. Three hours. Millie thought it was what she wanted, but she found the quiet nerve-racking. With the silence came time to think. Time to worry when she should be planning. But her mind was in chaos. And wouldn't you know it, that bastard Shadow read her like a book.

"You gotta get your head in the game, sweetheart. We can't go in there with demons lurking. Enough of those inside that place."

Demons. Apt word for it.

As she thought back, she remembered how it felt waking up in Shadow's arms. Right before her sister laid into them. She'd gone to sleep almost immediately the second he'd closed those brawny arms around her and slept like the dead until she woke up sprawled on top of him. Had she ever slept so soundly? Or gone to sleep so quickly?

She peeked over at the big man. He was huge. Tall and strong. His skin was a dark, deep carob color with scars crisscrossing his brawny arms. She hadn't seen the rest of him, but she could appreciate muscles playing under his shirt whenever he moved. His thighs filled out his dark pants to perfection. He was everything she'd ever wanted in a man and everything she couldn't have.

"I'm fine," she finally managed to say.

"Liar," he said, not missing a beat.

"OK, so I'm not fine, but we can't delay on this. If I'm right, Katya doesn't have even a day for delay."

"I thought Venus was the one to have spoken with a contact on the ground."

"She is. But if they've put Katya in that maze, they don't expect she'll be there long. Getting food and water to her will be difficult at best. She can't get in and out on her own, and Victor won't want her dying in his custody."

"It's been four years, Lyudmila. How do you know what he's thinking now?"

"Because that's why he built the maze. He likes games. Always did. He's a killer, but he doesn't like getting his hands dirty. Think of him as cat playing with mouse. He's probably told her she could go free if she made it out of the maze. Katya was always timid child. I tried to get her to be boisterous and lively, but our mother would stifle that side of her every chance she got. Like she wanted Katya to blend into background, beneath notice of her father."

"So you think it unlikely she'll even try?"

"No. She'll try. But she'll give up easily. Afraid of

getting lost."

"If Venus is right, it sounded like she got a message out to her contact somehow."

"That I could see. She was always very clever. She's nine now, though. I could have her personality pegged wrong. A lot can happen in four years to shape a person."

"Well, at least you've got your mind on Katya. Keep it there so all three of us can get back alive."

They watched the place for a long time after they got there. Consulting the maps and blueprints Giovanni had made them and deciding on the best way in and out.

"The problem with maze is that you have to go in one side and out another," Millie said. "I'll have to enter here" -- she pointed to the front side of the property --"and exit here," pointing to the back side. "Once outside, we'll be vulnerable to attack, as there is three-acre perimeter of cleared land around the place."

"Giovanni says the wall is just that. A high concrete wall. Getting over it will be a problem with no way to climb it, and you won't have time to destroy a section without blowing it up."

"Yes. But if we can get close to it, then run the perimeter next to it, we can slip under cameras and lights. You can meet us here." She pointed to a section of the wall a little more than half the distance from where she planned on entering. "You can drop rope and haul us up."

Shadow nodded. "Not a bad idea. The land slopes there so you'll be a couple of feet closer to the top of the wall."

"Exactly."

"How are you going to get inside?"

"Very carefully." She was going to kill the shit

out of anyone in her path. But she wouldn't tell him that. He'd just try to talk her out of it.

"Uh-huh. You know we have no backup if this goes sideways. Right?" Man read her pretty well.

"I do. You're just going to have to trust me."

"Babe." Shadow straightened from where they crouched over the map he'd pulled up on his phone. "You've got to know I only trust people I've worked with before that much. I know you will probably kill anyone you come across, but I need to know that's what you plan. We kill anyone here it changes the whole game."

She shrugged. "I won't kill anyone not in my way. How about that?"

Surprisingly, Shadow chuckled. "Little bloodthirsty thing. Fine. I can live with that." He looked back down at his phone. "Giovanni says the guard patterns are surprisingly routine and lax. They patrol at the top of the hour and are finished fifteen minutes later. We'll have forty-five minutes to get in, get the girl, and get out. Can you work with that?"

"Assuming he's not changed maze -- which would be very difficult -- then yes. I can get done in those guidelines. When is best time to go?"

"Give it another couple hours. Around two or three local time would be the best. It will be late, and they'll be more apt to make their rounds in a hurry so they can have a nap. Giovanni says they sometimes meet in a room to play cards or catch a little shut-eye."

"Does he have real-time feed?"

"Yes. He's sending me running messages about movement. They check your girl's immediate area -- the doors on either side -- at exactly twenty-one minutes past the hour. It's the last place they check before knocking off until the next patrol."

"OK, then." Millie sighed and stretched. "It's eleven now. If we plan on going in at two, will that work for you?"

"I think so." Millie watched as Shadow stood and stretched, too. She could see thick abs tenting his shirt as well as a defined chest. What would it feel like to run her hands over his body? To feel all that strength beneath her palms? God! Maybe Venus was right. Maybe she was a whore. Because she could totally see losing herself to this guy. Not her heart. Never that. But she'd love to find out how well his body could play with hers.

"Like what you see, sugar?" The man missed nothing. Millie's face heated at the knowing smirk on his face.

"Well, you're strong. Always a plus." She tried to play it off, but his knowing she'd been ogling him only made her mouth water to look at him more. In her life, she'd never had a lover. Not really. She'd never trusted anyone enough to explore that side of her nature. It hadn't kept her from looking at men -- or women. She appreciated the beauty of the human body in all its forms. But to trust someone enough to be that vulnerable to them -- mentally or physically -- wasn't something she was capable of. "But I don't mix business with pleasure."

"You afraid of proving Venus right?" His question was asked quietly, but she also heard a note of understanding in his tone.

"Venus has nothing to do with how I live my life," she snapped. "I simply don't trust you enough to do anything more than look."

"Uh-huh," he said, stepping closer to her. "That why you slept like a baby in my arms earlier? Don't seem like something a warrior would do. And, make no mistake, you're a fuckin' warrior, Lyudmila." He looked at her for long moments. Just staring at her. Looking for vulnerability in her eyes? "Yeah. You trust me," he finally said, straightening to his full height. "You just don't want to admit it to yourself."

With that, Shadow turned his back on her. Back to the truck, retrieving supplies and weapons for the operation in a few hours.

Chapter Four

Shadow's phone vibrated as someone called. He glanced at the screen and scowled. Giovanni. That couldn't be good.

"Yeah."

"Have you started operations yet?" Giovanni's tone was clipped.

Shadow sighed heavily. Running his hand over his face once, he glanced at the house several hundred yards in front of them. Nothing seemed amiss, but then Giovanni would be in a better position to know if there was a change in plan.

"No. We were waiting until two a.m. local time. Millie won't be leaving here for another hour."

"Well, hold up. You've got company."

Shadow put his field glasses to his eyes and gazed hard at the building before them. He could just make out two cars circling the drive. Both appeared to be the big, ostentatious luxury kind, signaling whoever was in them either had money or represented someone with money.

"Any idea who?"

"No. But it's a good bet they've come about the girl inside. I've been watching this place since you first came to me with it. No one's been in or out. Until now."

"You think they're taking her now?"

"This visit is likely about her, but I'm not sure they'll actually be taking her yet."

"Set up before the meet? Everyone feeling each other out?"

"Probably. Once they get inside I'll know more. I've tapped into audio as well as video on the inside." Giovanni's confident, clipped voice was oddly soothing to Shadow as he continued to gaze at the compound.

"Keep me informed. I'll tell Millie to hold up. She was getting ready to start her descent to the entry point. It's a long way down. She needs time to get in place."

"If they're really here for the girl now, you're going to need to track that son of a bitch."

"You send us something?"

"Yep. Got three smart trackers. They'll be in the box you set aside because you have no idea what to do with the stuff in it."

"Bastard," Shadow muttered as he moved to the back of a truck to look through the boxes. Sure enough, he found the container Giovanni was talking about. "Found them. How do we use them?"

"Just get one of them on each vehicle. They're magnetic. Only try to get them on a part of the car no one can see because they won't let go once they're attached. I'll do the rest."

Shadow snagged all three trackers and moved to where Millie was still watching the compound with her own field glasses. "Change of plan," he growled. "We need to get these devices on those two cars down there."

"I was just getting ready to leave for compound. What's going on?"

"Giovanni thinks whoever is in those vehicles may be here for Katya. If they are, we need to be able to track them. Either way we have to change our plans. You can't go inside and risk getting trapped in that maze with an unknown element inside the compound."

Millie looked like she might argue with him, then let out a breath. "Can't argue with that logic. Even if they aren't here for Katya, we need to know if is someone we need to hunt down later."

Shadow raised his eyebrows and grinned. "Bloodthirsty little thing, aren't you? I like it."

Millie rolled her eyes, but Shadow could see a grin tugging at her lips. "You're more than a little crazy. Most men would run screaming from me."

"Because you're a little bloodthirsty?"

"Because I can kick their ass and not bat eyelash. *Or* break nail." She smirked, referencing her earlier comment to Venus.

Shadow chuckled. "Much as I hate to admit it, the fact that you can kick my ass turns me on."

She gave him a wicked grin. "Much as I shouldn't admit it, your muscles and size turn me on."

"Not sure that's a compliment since I had nothing much to do with my size, but I'll take it." He tossed her one of the trackers. They were small and round. About an inch in diameter. "Giovanni says to stick them someplace not easily seen, but to be careful. Once they stick, they're stuck. And they're magnetic."

"OK. Stick round thingie on car. Meet around back of house?"

"Hum… not sure, babe. I don't want to get caught inside the perimeter if we have to wait long. I think it would be best to wait until their guests leave before going inside, and if they do leave with Katya, I want to be able to follow them. Giovanni will have the tracker and won't lose them, but we still need to be close."

"Good plan. What about if we meet on that ridge line, just above property?" She pointed out the spot she was talking about. It was dark, but with the infrared goggles, Samson could see what she meant.

"I think that would do. We should scout it first. If

there's not enough cover, we can come back here. Might have to postpone a rescue until tomorrow. I don't want to take a chance we get caught. Not only would we be in danger, but they'd move Katya, and we might not have an opportunity to rescue her."

She thought about that. "I don't like waiting another day."

"Me, either," Shadow said quickly. "But I'd rather take a little extra time and make sure we're not compromised. Giovanni has eyes on her either way. If the guests take her, we've got the car tracked. If they move her, Giovanni can still track her as long as she has those chips in her."

"What if they take them out?"

Shadow shook his head. "You think they would? Why go to the trouble of putting in long-lasting trackers if they can't leave them in? While they may take out one, assuming it's the explosive kind, they won't likely take out the other one. Putting trackers on the cars is merely a precaution. And to make sure we can find the bastards again if they need to die."

Millie thought about it for a long time, studying the layout once more while she thought. Shadow respected that. She really took her time to turn all situations over in her mind. She didn't just run into anything or insist on something simply because she wanted instant gratification. "I agree. Is best plan."

"Good. Then we'll deliver the little magnetic disks to the cars out front, then come back here to watch and wait."

"Your Giovanni is monitoring?"

"Continually. He has Alex's wife, Merrily, assisting. She's nearly as good as him."

"Ah," she said, visibly relaxing. "There's woman on duty. I feel much better."

Shadow let out a bark of laughter before covering his mouth. Last thing they needed to do was be made because he got mouthy. "Yeah. I like you, little Lyudmila. When this is over, I'm askin' you on a date."

She snorted. "Yeah. Let me know how that works out for you."

"I'm suave and smooth. It'll work out fine for me. You'll be charmed, and I'll get lucky." He winked at her.

"Venus will have fit. So, I doubt you'll be taking me anywhere. Let alone getting lucky." She checked her gun, chambering a round before standing. "Let's get this done. I'll feel better when Giovanni has good signal on cars."

"Yes, ma'am."

* * *

Placing the trackers took some work, but Millie managed to roll under each car and place the small disks on different parts of the undercarriage. In both cases, she chose nooks toward the center of the vehicle where they couldn't be immediately seen. She kept to the shadows and was quick. Shadow was close, but grudgingly agreed she was quicker and smaller and therefore better able to get the job accomplished and get out with a better chance of success. He seemed on edge the entire time while they waited for the right opportunity. He even growled occasionally before catching himself and shaking his head.

"You get in. Then out. You don't get distracted. I don't care if you see Katya herself walking toward you, you *do not* deviate from the fuckin' plan. You fuckin' got me?"

She'd wanted to snap a salute and say, "Sir, yes, sir!" just to piss him off, but she refrained. He sure wasn't acting like himself. At least, not like the person he'd presented to her so far. It was like his protective instincts had come out in full force, and he couldn't rein them in.

When she'd finished, Shadow practically dragged her back up the hill to their lookout spot. The overhang she'd spotted had several bushes that gave them adequate cover to sit back and watch until it neared dawn. The night was cold, and she was chilled to the bone. All she wanted was to curl up under an electric blanket and sleep for a fucking week. Instead, they lay in the bushes and watched their target.

They'd have to move back up to the Hummer before daybreak. Their ride had safeguards that would alert them through Shadow's phone if someone found it, and the thing would self-destruct unless he aborted the feature. Which she thought hilarious given that he'd refused to let her drive under the pretext of him not wanting it damaged.

"I think you're afraid of my driving," she said as they both gazed through the infrared field glasses at the house. It was a boring task, but one they needed to be careful about. She didn't take her eyes from the scope.

He was quiet for a moment, not moving. Millie was beginning to think he either was asleep in that position or was just not going to answer her when he finally responded.

"Why would you say that?"

"Hummer has self-destruct action you deliberately set to go off if someone finds it and you don't deactivate it within ten seconds. That just smacks of fear to me."

"Fear we'll compromise ExFil. That vehicle is owned by them."

"Yeah? If that's only reason you won't let me drive, why not just take a nondescript Chevy that makes less noise in woods. Eh?"

Again, he was quiet for a while.

"This is more reliable."

"Not if someone finds it and you destroy it."

"You ain't gettin' me to admit I'm scared of anything related to you, sugar."

"No? Then I'll stab you in leg on way out and I'll drive."

That got a snort of laughter before he tried to cover it with a cough. "You do, little girl, I'll spank your ass when we get back to Poland."

"Fuck," she muttered, not really meaning for him to hear, but the image he'd just painted was hot as hell. And, embarrassingly, she wasn't as opposed to it as she should have been.

He glanced at her, then went back to watching. "Got a feelin' I'm in for a long ride home with a knife wound in my leg." How the hell could he read her so easily? And what would he do with that knowledge? Hell, what did she *want* him to do?

Shadow's sat phone buzzed once, signaling a message. Hopefully good news from Giovanni. She wanted to get Katya out of that place tonight. She glanced at her watch. Four forty-five. Way too late to start this, but she wouldn't question it if Shadow said they were a go.

"Copy," was all Shadow said after thirty seconds of silence while he listened to whatever report he'd been given. Then he tucked the phone away and moved out of the brush where they'd lain on their bellies watching the house. "Come on," he said softly. "Back to the cage."

"Cage?" What was he talking about?

"Sorry. The Hummer. We call it a cage because it's not as free as a bike. It's enclosed. Can't feel the wind around you."

"Does it feel free when you ride bike?"

"Definitely. When we get back home, I'll show you."

"Might take you up on that."

He turned and grinned. Shadow was a man who smiled freely, but this somehow looked different. His whole face lit up. That was when Millie realized that his easy-going manner, his ready smile, his compulsion to help everyone get along was all an act. He was as shadowed as his name. Always on guard. He seemed like he was carefree, like he didn't have a care in the world, but it was all a facade. Underneath was something dark. Dangerous. And she found she wanted to explore that side of him.

They made it back to the base they'd set up about an hour before dawn. Millie was running on empty but refused to tell Shadow she needed sleep. They set up some devices around the perimeter. Shadow said something about them being an early-warning system Argent had devised for ExFil for just such cases. That way they could get some sleep, and Giovanni could warn them if anyone was too close. Though it was well into spring, the days could still be quite cold, especially on a cloudy day. Though the night had been clear, there was a thick cloud cover moving in, promising rain. Shadow confirmed it when he consulted Giovanni.

"Gonna be a storm moving in this morning. Expect tonight to be soggy."

"Great," she muttered.

"Don't like the rain?"

"I like it fine," she snapped. "Just not like this.

Climbing uphill will be dicey at best of times. Mud will make it even worse."

"Yeah," he agreed. "Was thinking the same thing." He opened the back of the Hummer. All the cargo had been stowed on either side where it was lashed down, leaving the middle free of clutter except sleeping bags, which were laid out now as if they were ready for sleep. "In you go," he said, picking her up by the waist and lifting her as if she weighed nothing.

"What are you doin'?" she squeaked. "*Der'mo!*"

He chuckled. "Just assistin' a lady inside." He crawled in after her. The sleeping bags had been unzipped so all they had to do was pull the top half over them once they'd lain down. Millie desperately wanted sleep, and she was so cold and tired, she was trembling with both. Any other time she'd have wrapped herself up in that sleeping bag in a little ball behind some of the equipment and just passed out, but this was different.

Shadow didn't bother pulling the top of the sleeping bag over him, nor did he remove his boots. After closing the back hatch, he set his phone within easy reach, put his hands behind his head, and closed his eyes. Millie sat there for a few seconds before pulling the sleeping bag over herself. She'd removed her boots first thing, knowing there was no hope of getting her feet warm if she didn't.

She turned her back to him, trying to ignore the big man with the body heat practically radiating from him while she huddled in her sleeping bag, shivering like she was dying of hypothermia.

"You should take your socks off, too," he rumbled beside her.

"What?"

"If you want your feet to get warm, take off your

socks."

"Why?"

"Sweat. Your socks are probably damp with it. Your feet'll stay cold until they're dry."

"Oh." It was an inane thing to say, but her brain was about to just shut down from fatigue. How long had it been since she really slept? In Poland, with Shadow? And that had only been an hour or so. It had been so long since she'd slept, and the inactivity was weighing on her.

She sat up and pulled her socks off, putting them in the tops of her boots so she didn't have to look for them later. "Not a good idea," she mumbled. "Will slow me down if we have to leave in a hurry."

"Don't you worry 'bout that none," he said, his American Southern accent prominent. She loved the sound of it. So smooth and welcoming. His voice was deep, and the timbre settled into her body and lulled her. She wanted to wrap herself up in his warmth and soothing appearance and just sleep for a week. But that was a dream. He was too close to her sister for her to start anything with him. As evidenced by Venus's reaction to them sleeping together. Even if all they'd done was sleep. "I'll take care of any of that."

"Was that Giovanni earlier?"

"That last call? Yeah. Said from what he was able to pick up, this was the first meet before your sister was turned over. They're supposed to leave this morning and return in two days. Apparently, they live ten hours out."

"They didn't fly?"

"Nah. Didn't want to log a flight plan, and this place is remote enough they'd have to land in a larger city. Guessin' it'd be easier to drive the girl out than to try to fly her. To say nothing of the paper trail."

"So we need to go for her tonight."

"Yes. Which means we need rest. How long has it been since you slept?"

She snorted. "Since Venus bit my head off."

He chuckled. "Yeah. I hear ya. Before that."

"Two? Days?"

"About what I thought. Sleep, sugar. I got your back."

Surprisingly, she did. She pulled the sleeping bag up to her chin, tucked her chin to her chest, then let blackness take her.

Chapter Five

When Millie woke up, Shadow was wrapped around her, her head pillowed on his big bicep. She was warm and comfortable, other than an urgent need to relieve her bladder. The very last thing in the whole fucking world she wanted to do was move.

Shadow nuzzled her neck, and she stretched automatically, allowing him better access. "Need the bushes?"

She barked out a startled laugh. "Yeah. Guess I do. What time is it?"

"Still early afternoon. One."

"We need to get up?"

"Nah. Still got at least eight hours. We both need to sleep while we can. Especially you. You're the one taking all the risks."

"Only doing what's necessary. Besides, she's my sister. My responsibility."

"She's a scared young girl. Which makes her someone we all want to help." He nuzzled her neck again. "You know, Giovanni said Merrily found the communication with Venus's contact in the FSK. She was very informative and level-headed. Giovanni found her by using the information she passed on. We all are looking forward to meeting her. We all want to help her."

"I didn't mean to imply no one wanted to help her, Shadow."

"You didn't. Just realize you don't have to do it alone. Venus should be here with you, yes. But you two need to put to rest this bad blood between you. You were both young when you escaped. As much as you wanted to save Katya, she wanted to save you both. She had you. There was no guarantee she could get Katya out without all three of you getting killed. Venus had to make a hard choice, and she chose to save the sister she had her hands on."

"I never thought of it that way."

"Yeah? You've got several hours to think about it now."

Millie brushed at her eyes where moisture had gathered. "I suppose I do." Taking a breath, she sat up. "I'll be right back. Need those bushes now."

More than the bushes, Millie needed to think. About Venus. About Shadow. While she knew she and her sister could mend their problems, she had no idea what to do with Shadow, or, more importantly, her reactions to him. He was… larger than life to her. There was a calming vibe that seemed to radiate from him, but also a hidden streak of violence underneath she sensed was just waiting to explode.

When she returned to the Humvee, she found Shadow leaning against the truck looking all casual. Millie knew in reality he was anything but.

"You waiting out here for me?"

"Just thought I'd get a little fresh air myself," he said, but Millie could see the way he relaxed the moment she was in sight. "Did a quick check." He raised his phone. "Everything's good."

"With your phone?"

"Uh, yeah." He opened the hatch on the Humvee. "Giovanni installed an app. Lets me monitor everything same as he does."

"He still watching, too?"

"Oh, yeah. But I'm not keen on leaving our protection to others. At least not all of it." He held out his hand for her and Millie took it. He helped her inside, climbing in behind her and closing the door. "We should be good for another few hours." Shadow lay back on the floor of the Humvee, once again putting his hands behind his head and crossing his legs. With a sigh he closed his eyes.

Millie removed her boots and socks as she watched Shadow under her lashes. Again, he seemed relaxed, but there was an air of something. Like he was waiting. Watching. Her?

When she lay back on the sleeping bag, before she could pull the top over her, Shadow rolled, wrapping his arm around her waist, scooting his other arm under her head to pillow it.

"Shadow?"

"Shh," he said, finding her neck with his face. "Like sleepin' with you like this."

Millie sighed. Trying to deny him would be futile. "I like sleeping with you, too."

Shadow pulled her in closer, tucked her against his body. With a sigh, she relaxed against him, bringing a hand up to his brawny forearm. His skin was hot. His body soothed the chill inside her. It also made her want more.

They lay like that for a long while. Neither spoke, but they didn't drift off. Finally, Millie turned over to face Shadow. She reached up and stroked his strong jaw. He raised an eyebrow.

"Whatcha want, sugar?"

"Will you kiss me?"

He grinned. "Been hopin' you'd want that." Rolling slightly, Shadow lowered his head to hers, his generous mouth taking hers gently, then with more fervor. Millie whimpered, gripping Shadow's shoulders tightly, pulling him more fully over her.

How far would he take her? Millie knew she wanted it all. For the first time in her life, she'd met a man who could make her feel more than a passing interest. The first time she'd seen him standing with Venus, she'd thought for sure her sister had a claim on him. She'd tried to ignore him even to the extent of ignoring a potential enemy, which she'd never done. Not since she'd left Belarus. But Shadow called to her on an elemental level. Even if he did belong to her sister, she had no idea how she'd resist him.

"Shadow," she whispered between kisses.

"Not sure what you're thinkin'," he rumbled, "but put it out of your mind. This is happenin'."

Millie cupped her hands around his face, forcing him to look at her. "Just tell me you have nothing to do with my sister."

He tilted his head to the side as if to process what she was asking him. "You mean, like a relationship?"

"Personal."

He leaned down and took her lips once more for a soft, slow kiss. Millie could feel the fire hadn't died down -- he simply held it back until he could unleash it again. That was the danger of Shadow. He could hold in all that aggression in a calm pool, letting it simmer just beneath the surface. When it finally forced its way through, it would do so with explosive fury. As much as Millie wanted that answer, she wanted to keep kissing him. To let him take her on a sensual adventure unlike anything she'd ever dreamed of. Because, if he admitted to having any kind of relationship other than strictly platonic, she knew this interlude would end. Regardless of what Venus thought of her, Millie would never let a man come between them. Not for something as frivolous as sex.

"Venus is a member of Salvation's Bane. I'm a member of Bones but am accepted in Bane since Bones is a sister club. I'm also friends with several of Bane's members, including your sister. But I have never had even one sexual thought about Venus." He chuckled. "She'd have my balls hangin' 'round my neck if she even thought I'd had a sexual fantasy about her. When we're back, you can ask her. She'll tell you that exact thing."

"Then why was she so upset earlier?"

"Couldn't tell you, sugar. Maybe it had something to do with how she thought you and Mikhail had something going on."

"She loved him," I said. "He loved her, too. But she was FSB. They are very careful who they single out as friends or family. As woman, she'd be expected not to marry, though that's not something that's actually spelled out. It's unspoken, yet they all know it. Very few women are let in, and certain measures are taken. At least, that's what we were told."

Shadow brushed a stray lock of hair off her forehead, rubbing the strands between his fingers for long moments as he gazed down at me.

"Tell me something, Lyudmila. Do you have a man in your life?"

She was silent for a long time. She didn't but was afraid to answer him. "My life is far from simple, Shadow. But no. There is no man. I don't wish there to be."

"Oh? And what about me? Hm?"

"Just because we play together now doesn't mean it's anything other than one-time thing. Or maybe just way to pass time."

That got a grin from him when Millie didn't even get the joke. "You think not?"

She blinked up at him. "No. We can fuck. Doesn't mean anything afterward."

He chuckled. "You keep tellin' yourself that, sugar. It means somethin' to me."

"You don't know me, Shadow." Something in her chest tightened. She wasn't sure if it was pleasant or unpleasant. Part of her wanted to run like hell. Another part of her, the part she never acknowledged, wanted to grab on to him with both hands and never let go.

"I know enough. Now. No. I haven't had sex with your sister and never intend to. She never indicated in any way she was interested in me. Given how closely our clubs are related, I doubt she would see me as anything other than a brother. So, tell me now if you have another objection. If not, I'm makin' you mine right here. Right now."

"Not yours, Shadow," she said with a shake of her head. Millie tried to make it firm, but even she heard the quaver in her voice. "You don't know anything about me."

"Don't need to," he insisted. "I saw how fierce you are. And I see how you're fightin' for your family."

"Venus and I are at each other's throats. So much so you wouldn't let her come when it was her operation in first place."

He waved that off. "That's all family stuff. Stuff anyone with brothers or sisters goes through from time to time. You'd never let anyone else mistreat her same as she'd never let anyone touch you. You'll work it out now that you're together again. I can see it in both of you."

"But --"

He silenced her with another kiss. This time, he let a little of that caged emotion free. He swept his tongue inside her mouth, catching every little gasp he coaxed from her. When he finally raised his head, he'd somehow maneuvered himself between her legs so that his hips rested in the cradle of her thighs. Millie could feel his rock-hard erection pressing insistently against her pussy through their clothes, and she wanted it inside her like she wanted her next breath.

"Tell me you don't want this, Millie."

She shook her head. "I do want it. But only here. Now. After? Is anyone's game."

Shadow gave her a hard look even as his lips quirked. If she didn't know better, Millie would have thought he was merely giving her a cocky grin. Like he knew he could make her come back for a repeat if he fucked her now. But she *did* know better. The longer she was around him, the more she learned his tells. Shadow was angry and determined. He wanted her. And he was plotting on how to keep her.

"Fine. I'll take what you're offering. Anything else we can discuss later."

"OK."

The second she said the word, Shadow descended on her with a conquering kiss. Before, she'd just thought he meant business. She could see how wrong she'd been. He stirred feelings in her she'd never known she had. Need. Lust. *Want...* She wanted this man. Not just for him to pleasure his body with hers. She wanted him for her own. A man who was strong enough to protect her wherever she went. Who would champion her causes just because they were important to her and help her see them through.

With a growl, Shadow worked her shirt up her body to whip over her head. She barely had time to gasp before he descended on her breasts. He lay on top of her, his weight pressing her into the floor of the vehicle. His big hands cupped both of her breasts through her sports bra and kneaded like they were the most exquisite tits he'd ever held in his hands. In reality, she doubted he could even tell they were breasts, they were so small and layered underneath in muscle.

Shadow shoved the elastic above her breasts and fastened his mouth to one nipple while his hand found the other and rolled and tugged while he sucked. Millie couldn't help it. She screamed in both shock and pleasure, arching her back to him as she cradled his head.

"Shadow!"

"Mmmm…" He hummed around her nipple, nipping with his teeth before rasping the flat of his tongue over the small sting. "Ripe berries," he murmured against her chest. "Fuckin' sweet as spring."

God, he was killing her! Shadow made her feel things she'd always thought were impossible. Men weren't for keeping. She'd always thought men were for scratching an itch when necessary but weren't good for much else. She'd been sixteen when she'd struck out on her own. Even then, she'd known better than to hook up with a man. Any sexual satisfaction she needed, she took care of herself. She was a woman alone. Giving a man control of her body was a sign of surrender. A flag she'd never even thought about waving. She'd seen what men could do to strong women. Her mother had given up when Victor had taken her. She'd become a shadow of herself. Millie had sworn that would never be her.

Yet, here she was. About to give her body to Shadow. And there was no way she was stopping. Even though she knew she should. He'd just said he wasn't letting her go. She didn't want a man in her life. Didn't need it. But Shadow intrigued her on more than one level. Besides, she wanted to see what happened when all that leashed and controlled energy exploded from him. It might not during sex. At least not like this. But she had the feeling she could get him to completely lose control if they were someplace he felt like he was safe doing so. She wanted that. Wanted the experience. More than anything, she wanted him to experience it, but only with her.

He bit down sharply on her nipple, making her gasp, her hands going to his head. She cried out, arching her back. The pain brought her back to the moment as well as threatened to send her body flying into a spiraling abyss where pleasure and pain morphed together until she didn't know which she desired more.

"Shadow," she gasped. "*O Bozhe*!"

"God got nothin' to do with it, sugar," he rasped. "Fuck, you're sexy!"

He continued to kiss and nip her breasts. Seemed like he couldn't get enough of her tits. The differences in their size should have at least made her uneasy, but the mere fact that his hands were so big he could nearly span her torso when he slid them up her body from her waist to her chest was a big fucking turn-on. Millie wanted all of this man. All of him. Any way she could get him. If that meant he feasted on her body at his leisure, she'd happily accept whatever he wanted to do to her.

"Gotta be careful," he whispered against her breast. "Ain't gonna scare a little thing like you into leavin' me after I fuck you."

"You could never scare me, Shadow." Millie circled his head with her arms. "*Moy voin. Moy moguchiy voin.* Do you have any idea what a fucking turn-on it is to have you over me like this? Love that you're so big and strong." She wiggled until she had one leg on each side of his torso. Then she bucked against him to get friction on her clit. Then she whispered in his ear, "*Trakhni menya, poka ya ne zakrichu*!" Fuck me until I scream…

Shadow jerked like she'd slapped him. Then he looked up at her, likely seeing the lust and want in her eyes. He met her gaze with a carnal desire that mirrored her own. Baring his teeth at her, he shoved down his pants before sitting up on his knees and yanking her own pants off her hips to her knees.

"You wanna scream? Want my cock fuckin' you so hard?"

"*Da*, Shadow! *Da*! *Posmotri na moyu mokruyu kisku*!"

"I see your wet pussy, sugar. Gonna taste it, too."

He did. Shoving her legs -- still with her pants around them -- to her chest, Shadow lowered his head between them and took a long, slow lick of her weeping cunt. Millie screamed, unable to hold back her reaction. It was the first time she'd ever had a man's mouth on her. She'd heard about it, read about it, but never thought she'd ever experience it. Maybe if the guy was kneeling before her, but no man she'd ever met would be willing to do that. And having Shadow kneeling in front of her while she either stood or sat didn't seem right. *This* was right. Shadow.

"Fuckin' sweet, girl," he growled. "So fuckin' sweet…"

"Shadow! *Bog*!"

When Shadow dug in to eat her pussy, Millie let herself go. She'd work out everything else later. Besides, she had no idea what Shadow's game with her even was. He pretended to want more with her, like he intended on something more than simply passing the time. But right now, she just couldn't think beyond sensations she'd never felt before.

"Mmmm... gonna eat you up." Shadow continued his sensual assault, driving her higher and higher, but never letting her fall. Millie screamed her frustration, but Shadow didn't let up.

Over and over, he brought her to the edge of madness, always leaving her just shy of her prize. When she struggled, pulling at his head, trying to get him to crawl up her body to sink his cock inside her and fuck her into oblivion, he resisted, but his growls and grunts grew louder and more insistent the longer he feasted.

"Please, Shadow! Please!"

"What do you need, *moy tsvetok*?" My flower.

"*Mne nuzhno priyti!*"

"Ahhh... My flower needs to come."

She nodded vigorously. "*Da! Pozhaluysta!*"

Finally, *finally*, Shadow moved up her body. Her legs were still trapped by her pants, but that didn't stop him. The next thing she knew, Millie felt his cock probing her entrance. Because her legs were pulled to her chest, she couldn't see. God, she wanted to see! She'd waited a long time for this. She should at least get to watch.

"Now, Millie," he said in that soft, Southern drawl of his. "You're mine."

Slowly, carefully, Shadow eased his way inside her. She gasped when he reached her barrier but said nothing. His gaze never left hers. The second he started to push through her innocence, Shadow paused. His eyes got wider, his mien determined.

"You're a virgin?" She gave him a little nod, not wanting him to stop, but unable to lie. "And you're givin' yourself to me now?"

"I am."

"Why?"

"Does it really matter? We're here. In moment. Don't stop, Shadow. Please!" The last thing she wanted to do was beg him for it, but she was beyond caring. She needed this like she needed to breathe.

"I wanna know why you chose me when you didn't let anyone else."

She thought about not telling him, but knew that would likely not get her anywhere. He'd just wait all fucking night to fuck her. "Because you're only man who's ever made me want sex this much." Her voice sounded small.

"Good," he said, as he sank into her ever so slowly. It was a stretch, but several long moments later, Shadow was fully embedded inside her pussy. He watched her so intently she wanted to squirm. His attention, along with the invasion of her body, were just two more things that turned her on. She loved that he took care with her, that he didn't want her to hurt. Because Millie knew he was on the verge of losing all that control. Maybe not completely, but he'd been about to ride her. Hard. "Now," he continued. "You're mine, Lyudmila. All mine."

She shook her head. "It's just this once."

"No," he said sharply, pulling his hips back before surging forward again with a measured thrust. "Not just now. Not just once. I'm your first. I'll be your only."

Then he moved. Slowly. In and out. Her legs were pinned between them. She wanted her pants off desperately but was afraid to move. Afraid he'd stop. Afraid he wouldn't.

"What do you want from me?" Her voice wavered as she spoke, a mixture of fear and desire. Fear for her heart if he kept insisting on keeping her.

Desire for the man she knew she wanted for her own.

As if he could read her mind, Shadow slid her pants the rest of the way off her legs and tossed them aside. Then he spread her thighs and lowered his weight on top of her. The weight of him pressing her into the floor was its own aphrodisiac. She cried out and gripped him tightly with her arms and legs. Her pussy ached where his cock invaded, but she was too far gone to ask him to let up. There was no pain, just a dull ache that was rapidly turning into the greatest pleasure she'd ever imagined.

"I want everything, little flower. Everything from only you." Then he kissed her as he fucked her in long strokes. Faster and faster. "I want your heart, Millie. I want your body. You're mine, and I ain't ever lettin' you go."

Just as he finished, Millie climaxed. She screamed, holding him to her and rocking her hips, rubbing her clit over his body to get the friction she needed.

"Shadow! *Bozhe moy, chto ty delayesh' so mnoy*!"

"Lovin' you, honey," he whispered in her ear. "Loving. You."

When she came this time, Shadow stiffened, his cock swelling inside her until he let out a long, loud roar. Hot cum spilled inside her, making her gasp and triggering another orgasm. She knew that probably wasn't a good thing, but she struggled to think of why. She'd known this man only a few hours, but she'd felt safer and more comfortable with him than she had any man in her life. He was a protector, and he'd put himself squarely in the middle of danger to help her save her sister. He'd even recognized she and Venus might not work well together, no matter how much they loved each other. Shadow was… a miracle. Her miracle.

They lay there for a long time. Shadow kissed her gently, nuzzled her neck. Her breasts. When he finally sat up, he reached for a packet of wipes and gently cleaned her, then himself before disposing of the used wipes in a plastic sack.

"I want you again, but you need more rest."

"What about you?"

He grinned before leaning down to kiss her gently. "I have a feeling I've had more sleep than you have over the last several days. You've still got dark circles under your eyes. I'd like to see them gone before we do this."

She ducked her head. "I guess I look bedraggled."

"Not at all," he said, reaching for her chin and forcing her to look at him. "You look absolutely beautiful. But as a soldier in my company, it's my duty to make sure you're as fresh for the fight as you can be."

"How long do we have?"

"Long enough for you to get a couple more hours."

"Are your club brothers watching everything still?"

He grinned. "Yeah. They think we need babysittin'."

She shrugged. "Then maybe we should both get some sleep." She'd never admit it but waking up to him holding her while she slept had been the most peaceful feeling she'd ever known.

Shadow glanced at his phone, shot off a quick text. When it dinged with the reply, he grinned. "Yeah, sugar. We can do that."

He handed her her clothes, and she put them

back on. All but her socks and shoes. Then he settled her with her head on his chest and pulled the sleeping bag over them. It wasn't long before Millie drifted off. No nightmares.

Chapter Six

The house was thrumming with energy. Millie lay on her belly where they'd perched on the landing in the bushes above the place watching. It was packed with people. Whatever had taken place, there was now a full-scale party going on.

"What do you think?" Shadow asked her opinion when Millie knew it wasn't in his nature to do so. He was a take-charge kind of man. As he'd proven to her earlier that day. The mere random thought of their earlier sex made her blush and had a goofy smile tugging at her lips. She cleared her throat and grunted before answering.

"Doesn't change plan," she said. "If anything, will be easier to get inside."

"Oh, yeah? How you figure?" Shadow didn't sound disbelieving or irritated with her assessment. Just genuinely curious.

"With as many people as there are in house now -- and there's got to be a couple hundred -- no way everyone knows everyone. We stick to plan. Same entry point. Your guy confirms she's still in same place, *da*?"

"Yeah. Says he sees her moving around, occasionally skirting the edge of the maze but never venturing far."

"Good. Only problem I see is exit. There may be people at exit door, even though no one can enter that way. I don't see Victor leaving door unguarded with so many people around."

"What do you want to do?"

"Stick to plan. We can communicate while I'm inside, *da*?"

"Wouldn't agree to this otherwise," Shadow

growled. His displeasure was evident, though she had no idea why.

"This is a bad idea," he muttered. Then heaved a sigh. "Fine. I'd say that, if things went sideways, you were to immediately abort and retreat, but I'd just be pissin' in the wind. Ain't gonna promise you I won't go in and drag your ass out with or without your sister, though."

"You won't," she said confidently.

"Oh yeah? Try me."

"You don't have it in you to abandon someone vulnerable and innocent. Especially not a child."

He muttered something she couldn't hear clearly but she was certain wasn't at all flattering. "Just get in there and do what needs doing. I've got you covered."

"Never thought you didn't."

"Just get in and out as quickly as you can. I'd hate to have to engage this thing and get us all killed."

"If is just normal party, most will flee at first sign of real trouble. Some will gravitate to fighting but not if they feel they are in danger."

"Good point," he said, surprising her. She'd have thought he'd argue with her. While Shadow was a really dominant guy, he took suggestions very well. Most men she knew didn't. "If it gets too hot, I'll launch a grenade on the southwest end of the house." He pointed in the general direction of where he indicated. "According to the layout, it's the farthest point from where Katya is being held. If that happens, I'll concentrate on that section. You'll have to give me constant updates, so I don't unintentionally bring guards down on the two of you."

"Understood." She stood, rechecking her body. She had room for two sidearms in shoulder holsters. Even those were questionable. "At some point. I might have to ditch my weapons."

"Place can't be that cramped. How would they get to her?"

"By dismantling the maze on the exit end."

"How do they feed her?"

"Unknown. There is hole in ceiling three stories up. My guess would be that way, but I can't be sure."

"Any way to just lift her up from there?"

She shook her head. "Room above it is where Giovanni says security command is. No way to take out that many people without raising all kinds of flags."

"Figured. Just making sure."

"We good?"

"As we'll ever be."

"I'll keep in touch with you in the maze and will talk you through the procedures I'm doing on Katya. I'll need you to keep me as up-to-date as you can on the situation outside the exit."

"Understood. Venus is watching, too. She'll be watching out for us as well."

Millie just nodded. She wasn't sure how she felt about that, but knew it was for the best. Actually, no. She felt better knowing her big sister was watching out. No matter how much Venus shot her down, made her doubt her own worth, Millie still looked up to her big sister. She was the one with all the training. She was the one working for an important global paramilitary organization. Millie was a scrappy little punk making her living in illegal street fights.

"Hey," Shadow said, gripping her shoulder. "What was that?"

"What was what?" Millie tried to play it off like it was nothing.

"That look. I saw it. If you're concerned about

Venus, don't be. She loves you."

She looked him straight in the eye. "No. She doesn't."

"Millie --" He tried to engage her, but she turned and took off down the side of the cliff. She had to rappel part of the way. It would be the most difficult part of getting Katya back to their ride. Putting all thoughts of Venus out of her mind, Millie made her way through the dense woods to her entry point.

"Two guards at the perimeter. That's it. Once you take them out, you're free and clear outside. No dogs."

"Must have put them up for the party," she said. "I'll take them one at a time."

"The one on the left should be going for a smoke break in five. That's been his routine."

"I'll start with him."

"You'll have two-and-a-half minutes to get it done. Then take the second one out."

"On it."

The first guy was so busy trying to dig his cigarettes out of his zipped sleeve pocket, he didn't hear her approach. She got him from behind, jumping up to wrap her arms around his neck and twisting hard before he had the chance to realize he was in danger. He dropped like a stone. Thankfully, she was strong. She kept him from hitting the ground hard and making enough noise to raise suspicion with his companion.

The second one was more aware of his surroundings. And he held his rifle like he knew how to use it. After a couple of minutes where Millie could see no way to take him unawares, she shucked her weapons and stumbled out of the shadows like she was drunk.

"What the fuck are you doin'?" Shadow hissed in her ear. *"What the fuck?"*

She stumbled once before bursting out laughing, then falling forward into the guy. He caught her on reflex, his arms tightening around her even as his gaze swept the area.

"You need to get back inside. How'd you get out here in the first place? Back of the house is off-limits." He spoke Russian instead of Belarusian, which was a big advantage to Millie since many Belarusians could speak and understand Russian but not the reverse.

She answered in a mix of the two languages. "Needed some air." She giggled. "Misha is very vigorous when he fucks me."

The guy gave her an annoyed look, obviously buying her drunk act. "You can't be out here. Go back inside."

With another giggle, Millie slid her arms around his neck, brushing her slight body along his. "I bet you could fuck me just as vigorously. All those muscles…" She rubbed her body over his chest, her words still a mixture of the two languages and very slurred.

The guy looked down at her with a mixture of annoyance and budding lust. "You need to go back inside," he said. This time he tried to speak in Belarusian after saying it in Russian but didn't quite get it right. The sentence came out muddled in the foreign language.

She stretched, her body rubbing against his sensually. "Big, strong, sexy man. You want to fuck my little pussy," she purred. Instantly, his dick went hard between them. His arms tightened on her, and Millie knew she had him. "I bet a big, strong man like you could give me all I want."

"Fuck you until you couldn't walk," he growled,

his Russian back. He didn't even try the Belarusian again. "Fill you so full of cum…"

Millie let him go, her fingers going to his pants button and undoing it. He wasted no time finishing what she'd started, dropping his rifle and shoving his pants and underwear down his legs. The second the rifle was out of his hands, Millie struck. Jumping and swinging herself around to the guy's back, she wrenched his neck as hard as she could. The crack was loud in the darkness. The guy dropped as easily as the first. Millie helped him to the ground again so there was minimal noise.

"They out of camera range?" she asked, not really knowing who was listening in but hoping Shadow could find out from the others.

"Move Romeo there four feet to the left into the shadow of the building," Venus instructed. Good. She could talk to Millie in real time.

"Be careful about it." Shadow's voice sounded tight, annoyed. Angry even. "Don't need you straining something before this even starts."

"Jesus, Shadow," Venus said. Sounded like she was probably rolling her eyes at the big man. "You sound like prissy school marm."

"Don't need your input beyond tactical information, Venus," he snapped.

"Someone's pissy this evening."

"Are the alarms for the doors disabled? I don't want to pick lock only to bring whole place down on me."

"Door alarms are confirmed down," Venus said. "Only cameras are active and they are spotty, thanks to Giovanni messing with them from the moment he found this place."

"They gonna expect anything?" Shadow asked

the question tersely. "Why didn't you guys inform us of this?"

"Because it wasn't something you needed to worry about since I'd already taken care of it." Millie didn't recognize that voice, but it was deep and masculine. And sounded vastly superior to all of them. She detested him immediately.

"Well, I need to worry about it now," she snapped. "How many cameras are glitching?"

"Enough," came the reply. "Each section is on a separate system. Since this area has frequent blackouts in both electricity and Internet, they have some of them working via satellite. When you get close, I'll cut off the electricity. Hope you brought a flashlight."

"Thanks for the heads-up, fucker," Shadow growled. "You know she's cramped on things she can carry with her. Ever think a flashlight might be a bit bulky?"

"I got this," Millie said as she picked up her weapons and fastened the shoulder holsters back to her body. "I don't need light to make it through."

"And if you get lost? If they changed something?" Shadow's voice was pitched higher now. Like he was about to lose his shit.

"It is real fear," she acknowledged. "But Victor is lazy at heart. If he thinks maze will hold her in and keep everyone out, there will be no need to change it. He has no idea I'm even on radar since I've been gone for four years. Trust me, Shadow. I've got this."

She heard him sigh over the connection. "Fine. But I'm going on the record as saying I absolutely do not like this. And, Giovanni, when I get back to the States, me and you are havin' ourselves a one-on-one conversation. In person."

"Over my dead body," Giovanni muttered.

"Exactly," Shadow spat. "Over your dead body."

"Would you two knock it off?" Venus bit out. "Not even in same room with either of you and testosterone is making it hard to breathe."

"Agreed," Millie said under her breath. She was concentrating on the door. Looking around, she saw only the one sensor, and the little red light that should indicate it was active was dark. Fuck it. She'd trust that prick Giovanni. "If he's wrong about any of security systems he's so casually declared inactive, Shadow, my last request is for you to kick his ass until he begs for death."

"Granted, sugar." Shadow's voice was deadly. Even the endearment he used didn't soften the tone.

She picked the lock in a few seconds and entered. Noise from the party in the front part of the house could be heard off in the distance. Louder than it had been outside, but still not enough to muffle her movements.

Surprisingly, she made it to the door to the maze entrance with only one encounter. That man was dealt with swiftly and stuffed into a nearby closet. As she opened the door, she took a deep breath. The room was dimly lit, and the maze panels were clear, giving security a good view of anyone entering or moving through the maze.

"Are cameras in this area off, Giovanni?" She hated asking the question, but, regardless of her earlier statement, she wasn't eager for Shadow to hunt him down. She wanted to get out of this alive with her sister safely at her side.

"They are. How long do you need?"

"Give me twenty minutes to get to center. If there are only two trackers, I hope to have them out and her stitched in another twenty. Then fifteen on the way out."

"So, an hour to be safe."

"Yes."

"I can manage that," Giovanni said. "Are you sure you can work in the dark? It's the only way to kill these cameras."

"I can. Once I get to Katya, I can use phone light. If worse comes to worst, I can just bandage her up and deal with the wounds later. I only worry about blood trail in case they use dogs."

"Try your best to stitch her up there. Should only take one or two stitches at most."

"Understood."

"Be careful, Millie," Shadow said. "Don't make me come in after you. You won't like it."

"Awww," she crooned. "My big man is so sweet."

"Don't make me puke," Venus drawled, sounding like it pained her hearing the exchange. "I'll get you a room when this is over. Just… yuck."

Millie couldn't help but smile but refrained from laughing.

"Bustin' your ass for that when you get back, little girl," he snarled.

She took a deep breath and entered the maze. The door clicked shut behind her, and she was trapped. The only way out was to navigate her way through. After the first few turns, she knew she was in trouble. Not because she couldn't remember the way, but because she was getting the horrible feeling of claustrophobia she'd always gotten when she forced herself to pretend to play in the maze. She'd always known that, if she got stuck, she was on her own. This time, however, if she got stuck, not only was she dead, but so was little Katya.

"You good, baby?" Shadow asked. "Your heart rate just spiked."

"I'm fine," she snapped. "Place is even tighter than I remember."

"Can you make it?"

"I will."

"Good. Tell me if you need anything. I'll give you a countdown every five minutes so you can gauge your time."

She grunted, not daring to talk more than necessary. Not because she couldn't or that she was afraid someone would hear her. Because she knew if Shadow heard even the tiniest waver in her voice, he'd come in guns blazing. No one would leave in that event.

The turns and narrow corridors of the maze seemed to be the same. But she was slightly larger than she was at fourteen and fifteen. There were several places she was mashed up against the front and back wall. More than once she nearly had a panic attack thinking she was well and truly stuck.

"Ten minutes to the center," Shadow called out softly in her ear.

"Copy." Her answer was clipped. Sweat poured from her skin, making her clothing damp with it. Once, she got stuck in a corner. The edge was sharp, and she was mashed against the opposite concave section. One of her guns got stuck, and she couldn't get the other hand near it to either adjust the weapon and push it out of the way or unclip her shoulder holster altogether. She wanted to scream in terror but managed to hang on to her sanity by a thread.

"Millie," Shadow's voice was in her ear again, a soft command. "Talk to me."

"I'm stuck," she admitted. "Gun is hung on

corner, and I'm wedged in tight."

"I take it you can't release the weapon or the holster?"

"*Nyet,*" she confirmed, trying to keep her voice steady and get her breathing under control.

"Can you retreat slightly until you're free, lose the gun, then try again?"

She did as Shadow instructed, knowing she should have already tried it. At first, she wasn't sure she was going to be able to move, then she managed to wiggle free and back out of the corner. It was still tight, but she was able to release the shoulder holster so that it fell to the floor when she moved back into the corner. This time, she was able to slide around and into the next long corroder.

"I'm through," she gasped out. "Moving on."

"You're good. Just take a second," Shadow said, his tone soothing. "You've got another ten minutes to keep on schedule."

"I won't need that long," she said, trying to inject confidence into her voice. "This was worst section. Was reason I knew I had to be careful with what I took with me."

"You still have the stuff you need to get the trackers out of Katya?"

"*Da.*"

"Good. You'll breathe easier when you're out in the open."

She didn't answer but got moving again. Not long after, she slid free of the maze into the open. Stumbling in with a gasp, she sank to her knees and just breathed for several seconds. Then she heard a little whimper.

Millie rolled over, scanning the area but unable to see anything. The maze she'd navigated from memory. Even in the light, it was so close and cramped, the only way to navigate it was from memory. Now that she was in the open, she needed a light to get her bearings.

Reaching for the phone next to her skin in the front of her sports bra, she called out. "Katya?"

"Who's there?" Katya's voice wavered in fright. She spoke in Belarusian. Not Russian. "Go away!"

"It's me, Katya. Millie."

There was silence, then Millie heard her shuffling around. She had the phone light on but turned to face the wall where Millie had just come from. It gave off some light so they could see but didn't blind her.

Finally, she spotted Katya. The girl was dressed in a plain, white, short-sleeved dress that came to about mid-calf. A sacrificial garment if ever there was one.

"M-Millie? But how…?"

"Your message got through to Venus. She found me."

Katya rushed to Millie, throwing her body into her older sister's arms and sobbing into her neck. "I was afraid I'd never see you again! You guys left me!"

"I know, honey," Millie said, wanting to cry just as hard as Katya was but knowing she had to keep it together. "I know, I know, I know." She took a breath, clutching Katya tighter to me. "I'm here now, though. And I'm getting you out of here."

"But the maze --"

"Don't worry, honey. I memorized it when Victor was building it."

"I'm afraid I'll get lost in it." She was quiet, but genuinely distressed.

"I'll get you out. I'm not leaving here without you this time. Never again."

"Do you swear?"

"I swear on my life, Katya. I'm never leaving you alone again."

"Lyudmila," Shadow's voice was a purr of menace in her ear. "Less talk. More gettin' the fuck out."

"I need to scan her. Find the trackers."

"You've got seven minutes. Get to it."

Katya whimpered when Millie told her what she had to do, but nodded. "I know where they are," she said, pointing first to her upper arm. Using the phone, she pulled up the app and scanned her arm. Sure enough, a little beep sounded. The chip wasn't deep. When she touched the area, Millie could feel the outline of it just under her skin.

"This shouldn't be too hard," she said in English, more for Shadow than for Katya. "Just need to numb it up a little."

Katya was brave while Millie did what she had to do, not moving or flinching when she administered the numbing medicine. One little cut, and Millie was able to pull the chip out in one piece. The wound bled, but a thick dressing and some tape stemmed the flow.

"I'll check it before we leave. May have to put another dressing on it. Definitely don't have time to stitch it."

"Just bandage it and do the sutures after we get back to base."

"Understood."

"Who are you talking to?"

She smiled at her sister. "A friend of mine. Venus brought him. You'll like him. His name's Shadow." She took a breath. "Now. Do you know where the other one is?"

Instantly, Katya sobered. She swallowed, slowly

moving one finger to her temple. Dread seized Millie's heart. If they'd embedded that chip in her brain, there was no hope.

As she looked, however, she thought she might sag with relief. "Is it just under the skin?" Millie asked. When Katya nodded, Millie moved the phone over her head slowly. It only beeped at the exact spot Katya had pointed to. Moving her finger over the spot, Millie nodded. "Right there. I feel it."

"Where is it, baby?" Shadow asked.

"Just under the skin at her temple."

"I'm betting that's the explosive one."

"I'm afraid to do this," she said. "What if I poke too deep?"

"You can do this. You've already done it once. Didn't Chase make you dig into his forehead?"

"No, that was Caesar. That is, Caesar made me cut into Chase's forehead because Chase was being a dick."

"Can't say I blame him. Chase can be a dick on the best of days." Shadow chuckled. The sound settled Millie when nothing else could.

Millie took a deep breath, meeting Katya's trusting gaze. "I have to get this out, Katya. I'd leave it until we got back to base, but I can't. Can you hang with me for little while longer?"

She nodded slightly several times. "I can do it."

After she'd changed out the needle on the syringe, she numbed an area at Katya's temple. The little girl closed her eyes tightly but didn't move after that. Millie opened the other scalpel and another set of tweezers before changing her gloves, like she'd been taught. Opening another set of sterile gloves, she put them on, then took the scalpel to make the incision, then carefully slid the chip from under Katya's skin before dropping it next to the first chip.

"Got them," she said, as she quickly got another bulky dressing and taped it to Katya's temple. "That will have to do," she said. "How much time?"

"You've got another five minutes before you have to go into the maze to keep to your original schedule. You've got five minutes of padding after that."

"Ok." She looked to Katya. "You ready to get out of here?"

The girl touched her temple and the bandage there once. Then she nodded. "I don't want to stay here, Millie."

"You're not, honey. We're leaving. Just hold on to me as best you can. It will be tight in a couple spots, but if we're careful, we can do this." There was no need to pack up the trash. She had no place to store it, and the trackers had to stay there. "Are trackers still giving off signal?" she asked Shadow, hoping everything was still good.

"Giovanni says you're golden. Just get the fuck outta there."

"Can he tell how many guards are waiting for us at the exit?"

"He's working on that now. Get moving."

She looked at Katya and nodded once. Then they entered the maze again.

Chapter Seven

"She's gonna have a shit ton of company," Giovanni said in Shadow's ear on a separate channel. Giovanni had set Shadow up to be able to talk to him and Venus without Millie being able to hear in case they needed to problem-solve while she needed to concentrate. Like now. The image he'd given Shadow showed at least eight men outside the exit. Not close, but there would be no way for her to get outside without being noticed. Once she and Katya were noticed, they'd sound the alarm. Shadow was up and moving the second the words were out of his mouth.

"I'm headed that way," Shadow informed Giovanni.

"Go in the way she did. You can get around to the exit of the maze with little problem if you're careful. Just take out one guy at a time."

"I have suppressors in my guns, but even those will make noise."

"Try to kill as many as you can up close, but don't take too many chances."

"If I draw too much attention, they'll double down on the exit to that fuckin' maze."

"If you get killed, you can't help them. Even if she has to fight for a little while, you can get her out if you stay alive."

"You got a drone armed and circling?"

"I do. Say the word, and I'll provide your diversion."

"Not 'til I say." Shadow wasn't sure he trusted Giovanni to hold off until he gave the word, but he hoped he'd let Shadow have the last say since he was the boots on the ground.

"Roger," Giovanni said.

Shadow hurried to the entrance and opened the door. Giovanni guided him through the massive house. He ran into several guards, whom he disposed of easily. The closer he got to his destination, though, the thicker the crowd. Still, Shadow fought his way through. He made as many closeup kills as he could, breaking necks or slitting throats. He needed quick kills that weren't messy, so he tried to keep it to the former. Soon, it wasn't possible.

"Stop pussyfootin' around and get it done, Shadow!" Venus snapped. "Shoot the motherfuckers!"

"Do it, Shadow!" Giovanni's voice was a whip.

He knew they were right. He just wanted to give Millie the time she needed. "Where are they?"

"At the exit," Giovanni said. "She's exiting now. There are six guards nearby."

"How far away am I?"

"A hundred feet."

Shadow took out his sidearms and started shooting. Even with the suppressed firepower, the noise was distracting. No way the guards didn't know something was coming their way.

"Need that distraction now, Gio."

"In five. Four. Three…"

Two seconds later there was a deafening explosion. The building shook and dust rained down. Shadow gave up all pretense at being quiet, shooting or stabbing anyone in his way. His only goal was to get to Millie.

It wasn't long before he heard Millie's battle cries. Then he spotted her. She was a blur of motion, taking out one man after another. Shadow shot two men headed in their direction before shooting one directly in front of him.

"Millie!" he shouted as he barreled ahead.

"Millie! Shoot the bastards!"

She didn't acknowledge him but took out the one gun she had left and pulled the trigger. The sound was like a thunderclap in the darkened house. Gunfire could be heard off in the distance, probably heading to the explosion set off by Giovanni's drone.

They killed the last two just as Shadow reached her side. He felt wild. On the verge of a killing rage. "Where's Katya?"

"Over here." Millie went to the corner where her sister huddled and pulled the child to her feet. "Come on, honey. We've gotta get out of here."

"She OK?"

"Yes. Her incisions need to be stitched. One at her temple is starting to soak through bandage, but I think she's fine."

"I'm scared," Katya whimpered.

"I know, baby. But Shadow's here. He'll get us out of here."

Shadow felt his chest expand even as the pressure and rage he felt mounted, trying to break free the monster inside him. It had been years since the monster had been this close. Never had he wanted to let it free more than he did right now. Anything to keep Millie and Katya safe.

"Quickly," Giovanni said, this time speaking on the open channel between Millie and the rest of them. "Go back the way you came. Everyone is gravitating toward the diversion."

"Let's go," Shadow said, urging the girls back the way he'd come. Millie picked up Katya, the little girl wrapping her arms and legs around her sister. Shadow led the way. "You stay on my fuckin' six, Millie. Don't get in front of me, don't get beside me. I have to know where you are at all times."

"But --"

"No buts!" he roared as he continued on. "On my fuckin' six!"

She didn't answer, but he knew she'd comply. If for no other reason than she knew it was safer for Katya.

By the time they got out of the compound, guards were moving back to the house, realizing the explosion must have been a diversion. "Gio? Can you drop another one?"

"Negative. Only have one drone with one payload. If you keep going the way you're going, you'll be intercepted just before you get to the cliff where you rappelled from."

"Is the campsite still secure?"

"Affirmative. No one's spotted it. Head that way and be prepared for company."

"How many?"

"Ten to fifteen," Venus said.

They ran as hard and as fast as they could, trying to get just that little bit ahead of the coming mob. Once they reached the cliff, Shadow knelt and readied his weapon, making sure they were fully loaded and that he had full clips at the ready.

"Get her up that fuckin' rope!" he bit out.

Shadow wasn't sure what Millie said to Katya, but she managed to get them started up the cliff when the first wave hit. Bullets whizzed by. He felt the wind off a few of them and marveled that he hadn't been hit yet. One did kiss his upper arm, the burn making him grunt in pain, but not stopping him. He knew he'd hit more than one, but many others took cover, firing at him from the safety of bushes and trees. Too many.

When they charged, there had to have been eight or ten coming straight at him. Shadow heard a noise in his head, trying to give him instructions, but all he really heard was a buzzing background noise to the battle he was engaged in.

He gave a battle cry, launching himself at the closest enemy, killing him almost instantly with a crack of his neck. Two more he shot. Then a third before a fourth was on him. Shadow stabbed him several times in the kidney before getting in four stabs to the throat, dropping the guy.

Just as he was lunging for another guy, a shot rang out above him, dropping the guy nearest him. A pause, then another shot, dropping another attacker. Shadow continued to pick off men as they stepped into the clearing, but the rifle above him was getting just as many.

With an unholy roar, Shadow threw himself at another attacker. This time Shadow tackled him to the ground and *pounded* the guy. Grunts and yells filled the air, followed by the sound of flesh hitting flesh. He got in a good punch to Shadow's kidney before Shadow punched his face over and over. Blood splattered up his arms. Over his chest. His face. Then he threw back his head and roared again, the beast finally slipping his leash.

* * *

There were no more guards following them. She and Shadow had killed every single one who had followed them up to the clearing, but Millie was under no illusion they were all Victor had in that house. From what she could see, the party was dispersing at an alarming rate. Cars peeled out of the parking lot while shots were still firing inside the house. Shadow was still on the ground beating the living fuck out of the last guy, but they had to go. *Now*.

"Shadow," she called, the mic no doubt picking

up her voice and piping it into Shadow's ear even as she yelled from the ledge. "Shadow!"

"He's in some kind of rage," Venus said.

"I'm going down," Millie said, setting her rifle aside and readying the rope to rappel.

"Millie?" Katya huddled in a bush, cold and terrified. "Please don't go."

"I have to, sweetie. Shadow needs me."

The girl looked from Shadow's hulking form on the ground, then back to Millie. "You'll come back?"

"Absolutely, sweet girl." She leaned in to hug her sister. "I'll be right back. You stay here. No matter what. Don't make a sound until we come for you."

"OK," she acknowledged, nodding.

When Millie looked up, Shadow still hadn't let up. But to be fair, the other guy was still fighting him. Somewhat. "Shadow!" No response.

Then she heard another voice on the channel she didn't recognize. "Shadow! Snap out of it! You have to get the woman and the girl out of there!" The only response was Shadow roaring again before he continued to beat on the guy under him.

"I'm going to him."

"No!" That same voice snapped. "He could kill you in this state! He's got to come out of it on his own!"

"We don't have time for him to come out on his own! It's not going to be long before this place is swarming with Victor's goons!" She didn't wait for a response but strapped on her gear again and slid down the line to the ground.

"I'm telling you to let him be, girl! He'll never forgive himself if he hurts you."

"He can't hurt me," she snapped back. "I'm better fighter than he'll ever be!"

"Millie," Venus pleaded as Millie unhooked herself. "Maybe is not such good idea?"

"I know what I'm doing, Ulyana. For once in your life, trust me. I'm not reckless or stupid."

"I know," she said softly. "I just don't want to lose my sister now that I've found her again. Either of them."

"You won't. I swear."

Once she reached the ground, Millie readied her weapon, easing up beside Shadow. Not close enough he could reach her without moving purposefully in her direction. She wanted to be close enough to penetrate the haze of rage he was in but far enough away to prevent herself from being collateral damage.

"Shadow!" She yelled his name. He simply bellowed louder at the top of his lungs as he continued to beat the man beneath him. The guy had stopped moving, and Millie was sure he was dead. This was a post-traumatic rage if ever she saw one. She'd had them herself from time to time, though not this bad. It was like, any time she got really hurt, something beyond what she was afraid she could get out of, she panicked. If she panicked, she fought even harder. But that only scratched the surface of what Shadow was now going through. He needed to know he was not alone. "Shadow… *moya lyubov'*…"

Immediately he whipped his head around. Instead of softening him, of bringing him back to the here and now, back to Millie, he snarled at her. "Not your love!" he bit out. "You don't want me beyond a fuck in the back of a truck!" Voicing that thought was more than he could handle. Shadow threw back his head and *roared*.

"So? When did you ever let that stop you? I thought you wanted more with me." Millie was undaunted. She could handle this. She could take Shadow's worst and not run. Hell, she wouldn't even flinch.

"Do," he said, shaking his head as if to clear it. He got to his feet from where he'd been kneeling over the man he was beating to death. A rage still burned deep, but Millie could see his struggle. He was fighting hard. For her. He took a step toward Millie. "I'm a killer." He waved his hand at the carnage behind him. "You don't want a killer in your life."

"Why would you say that?" She tilted her head, genuinely confused. "You think I've not killed? I've killed opponents in fights like the one where you found me. Some on purpose, because they deserve it. Some accidentally, when they were winning and instinct took over. I try not to, but it happens." Millie knew she was getting through to him. He was still riding a fine edge, but she was getting there.

"You saw what I just did! I get in a rage and can't control myself! My temper was always hot on the best of days. Things happened in war or when I was sent with ExFil to do a job and sometimes, when backed into a corner, I can't control the rage!" He yelled at her, looking frustrated she couldn't see that he was so close to the edge of madness.

"So? Neither can I. We'll work on it together."

He took another step toward her. Millie didn't back down, but she didn't move forward either. Shadow had to come to her on his own.

"My ex filed a domestic violence charge on me, Millie. No one knows it but Cain and Stunner."

She shook her head. "She might have accused you of abuse, but you'd never hurt a woman. Not like that." The longer he talked to her, focused on her, the more she could see Shadow getting a grip on himself.

"You sure? The law wasn't so forgiving."

Millie did go to him then. "Then they were fools. Your protective instincts are off the chart. No way you hit a woman. Not with your size and strength. You're always so careful. Even of me, and I can kick your ass in the ring no problem."

That got a chuckle out of him, and he closed the small distance still separating them, pulling her into his arms. "You're a fuckin' miracle, Lyudmila. Just a Goddamned fuckin' miracle." She had him back. She'd helped him work through his rage just like she knew she could. They were meant to be together.

"Let's get back to truck and get out of here. Katya needs to get out of here and we need to get back to Poland before anyone finds mess we made."

"Where is she? Did I scare her?"

She shrugged. "Not sure. But she's made of sterner stuff than you think. She made it out of that fucking maze without much more than a whimper. She saw me kill. If she's not running from me, I doubt she'll run from you."

Shadow chuckled. "Honey, you're five foot nothing and maybe a hundred pounds. I'm six feet nine and three hundred pounds. More of me to be scared of."

Millie shoved away from him. "Just because I'm short doesn't mean I don't pack punch! I can still take you in a fight. Fair or otherwise."

"Not sure about that, sugar. Physics apply."

She bared her teeth at him. "When we get out of here, I'll prove to you I'm right."

"Sure. Just make sure there's Jell-O involved, and I'm your man."

"Ooohh!" Millie stomped off, not really mad. More relieved. The old Shadow was back. She'd taken him completely out of whatever hell he was in and brought him back to her. She'd figure out the rest later. Starting with the past he'd revealed to her.

* * *

The rage and fear roiling inside Shadow was hard to control. Even once they were in Poland and the relative safety of the ExFil camp, he couldn't get rid of the excess energy. It rarely got this bad, but the fight outside that bastard's home had been one for the ages. On any normal occasion, it wouldn't have been a big deal. He had guns. He could use them in that kind of situation even if they were in stealth mode. But he'd had the women to protect. One of them only nine years old. Yeah, he was well aware Millie could take care of herself and her sister, but he'd staked a claim on her, and his mind refused to let it go. Looking back, he had no idea how he could have ever mistaken what he'd felt for Carrianne as anything close to love. Hell, he hadn't even been that possessive of her. He'd liked the idea of her. A woman of his own. But he hadn't loved her. There was no way he could say the same thing about Millie.

Cain had debriefed him the second they'd gotten out of the Humvee and into the camp. The satellite link had been active and waiting on him. The conversation hadn't been all sunshine and rainbows. His boss was concerned about him but tried to mask it with anger. Shadow had taken his dressing down without a word and acknowledged he'd deserved it. Had Millie been a less than courageous woman, Shadow might have lost his Goddamned mind for more than one battle. That was what bothered him the most. He'd put Millie in more danger than she would have been in if he'd just remained calm and taken care of business.

"Hey." Speak of the devil. Millie had showered

and changed. She wore a black leather halter with black leather pants and combat boots. The pants were open up the side and had leather laces holding the legs together. All the way to the waistband. Yeah. No way for panties there. Maybe she had on a micro thong. As he took in the visual, Shadow rubbed a hand over his mouth. "Cain offered me a ride on next ExFil transport going out. You staying or going?"

"If you're goin', I'm goin', sugar."

She smiled brightly. "Well, get move on. Car leaves for boat in hour."

He chuckled, "Boat, huh?"

"Yeah. Not getting on plane willingly."

"How did you score that?"

"Don't know. Don't care. Cargo ship leaves out of someplace north of here." She shrugged. "Cain said he'd get me lift and passage. I didn't ask questions."

"What about Venus and Katya? They goin' with ya?"

"*Nyet*. Venus wants to get Katya back to U.S. as quickly as possible. I agree with her."

"Don't you want to go with them?"

"I can meet up with them later." She tried to act like she didn't care, but Shadow could tell she did. She was ashamed of her fear of planes but was trying not to show it.

"How about if I go with you?"

"Kinda hoped you go with me on boat," she muttered.

"Sugar, if that's the way you want to go home, I'm there. I just want you to be with your sisters if you want. And I know you want." He reached out a hand to her. "Trust me to take care of you?"

Millie looked put out. Like she wanted to grumble and sulk, but she took his hand. "Fine. But if we crash, you and I are going to have conversation."

This time, the plane wasn't a cargo jet. It was a private jet, destined to stop in London, then on to Lexington, Kentucky. From there, Cain had a charter flight ready to take them to Somerset, Kentucky and a cage waiting to go to the clubhouse.

At the moment, they were sitting in the most luxurious plane Shadow had ever imagined, waiting for takeoff on the first leg of the journey. Millie was belted into the seat next to him, her eyes tightly shut, her hand gripping his in a death grip.

"I think Millie's scared of flying," Katya said in her lightly accented English. Apparently, the girl spoke Russian like her sisters.

"I am not!" Millie snapped, her eyes never opening. "I just like Shadow to think he has reason to coddle me. I like being coddled."

Katya giggled. Millie broke out in a sweat.

"I think I can manage that." Shadow chuckled, bringing Millie's hand up to his lips for a brief kiss. "In fact, the second we level off, I'm taking her to the back to help her relax."

Venus rolled her eyes. Katya giggled. "Does that mean you're going to kiss her? Because I think she wants you to kiss her."

"Oh, yeah. I'm definitely gonna kiss her."

Venus made a gagging noise. "So disgusting."

"I think it's sweet," Katya said, her smile fading. "I wish I had someone looking out for me like Millie does."

Instantly, Shadow was on alert. This girl was hiding the trauma she'd been through. Just like her sisters tried to. "Sweetheart, the second we get to the Bones compound, I'll find you a brother to watch out for you," Shadow promised. "You ain't got to worry about that from here on out. When Venus or Millie can't be with you, I'll make sure you have your very own bodyguard."

"There," Venus said, putting an arm around her sister and hugging her close. "You see? You'll never be alone again."

Katya looked up at Venus with such trust and hope in her eyes, it nearly made Shadow look away from the intimate moment. "I don't want to be scared anymore," she said softly.

"You leave that to us. Shadow and Millie will help me find guard for you, and he'll never let you out of his sight. You'll be sick to death of him before you're comfortable enough to be on your own."

"But what if I don't ever want to be on my own?" Katya looked at Shadow. Not at either of her sisters. Shadow thought it was telling. Girl was probably embarrassed but still terrified, though she was hiding it well.

"Sweetheart, you listen to me," Shadow said, leaning forward to really get the child's attention. "You don't want to be on your own, you ain't gotta be. Ever."

"Even when I'm grown up?"

"Nope. Not even then. You can't find someone on your own to be with you, I know three whole clubs of men who'll go on a hunt to find you exactly the right one."

"No one wants to do that." She sounded small and vulnerable, and it tore at Shadow. He rubbed his chest, trying to relieve the ache. Which was when Millie put her other hand over his hand holding hers.

"Baby, believe me. Those men are all gonna put you under their protection. Just like they have several other girls who've been through rough patches. That means, they're gonna have to approve any guy you want to be with in the first place. You can't choose? They'll be happy to choose for you. And why are we even talkin' 'bout this!" He scrubbed a hand over his face. "You're too young to date. Or have a man of your own. Or to think about kissing!"

That got her to giggle a little, before she sobered once more. "You were protecting Millie. Down there. In woods outside maze."

There was no way to hide his wince. "Yeah, sweetheart. I was protecting Millie. And you. I'm sorry if I scared you."

"Oh, you didn't," she said adamantly, shaking her head, her eyes round and wide. "You killed bad guys. They were trying to put me back in maze. Victor said he was gonna give me to someone. He said I had to be good and do what man said or I'd get hurt."

"Ain't no one gonna hurt you now."

"Do you swear?"

Shadow smiled. "Yeah, baby. Me and your sisters will always keep you safe."

Millie sniffled. Venus didn't even try to hide that she was wiping tears from under her eyes.

"I left you once," Venus said, taking a shuddering breath. "Was biggest mistake of my life. Second was not letting your sister talk me into going back for you." When Katya gasped and looked up at Venus with hurt in her eyes, Venus carried on. "I tell you this now because I don't want you thinking Lyudmila had anything to do with it. She tried to get me to go back for you, but I was afraid if I did, I'd lose both of you." Venus looked at Millie, stark pain etched on her ethereal face.

"I could have tried to go back for you at any time after that," Millie said softly. "I didn't because I was afraid I couldn't do it by myself. Then everyone who died trying to help us get out would have died in vain. After that, I was too caught up in hating Venus to figure out how to make it right and get you out." Millie undid her seat belt and slid to the floor at Katya's feet. She took her younger sister's hands in hers, squeezing tightly. "I was wrong. I came when Venus found me so hopefully that helps make up for it. But understand, I'll never let anything more happen to you. Victor will die someday, and I hope to have a hand in it."

"Victor's gone home," Katya said softly. "Back to Russia. Is why there was party going on. His new girlfriend missed being center of attention." She wrinkled her nose delicately. "I heard her and Victor arguing right before he put me in maze. She wanted me gone, and Victor agreed to give me away now, so Sasha didn't have to put up with me. He put me in maze because I tried to run after I heard them."

"We'll still get him," Shadow said seriously. "Maybe not right away, but he'll pop his head up soon. When he does, we'll be ready."

"Absolutely we will." Millie pulled the girl into her arms, hugging her fiercely. "Never again, *mladshaya sestra*. I'll never leave you again."

"*Ya tebya lyublyu*, Lyudmila," Katya said, hugging her sister as hard as Millie hugged her. "*Spasibo* for coming for me." She turned to Shadow. "*Spasibo.*"

"You're welcome, little one."

Once the plane leveled off and Venus had Katya settled into the movie *Frozen*, Shadow snagged Millie's hand and pulled her back to the cabin in the back of the plane. Inside, there was a small bed and a private lavatory.

"Bed?" Millie giggled. "Am I about to join mile-high club?"

"Absolutely. Can't havin' you thinkin' I can actually keep my hands off you."

The second the door was closed, Shadow pulled her into his arms and kissed her. Millie melted against him, smiling as she wrapped her arms around his neck. "I can't keep my hands off you either," she admitted. "After everything we went through down there, I need you, Shadow."

Shadow shivered in her arms, his hold on her tightening, afraid someone would try to take her away from him again. "I can't think about that right now, baby. Not now. Later."

"It's fine. Take what you need from me. I'm here."

"Fuck," he bit out, whipping his shirt off while she did the same with her own. "Fuck!" He hoped the fuckin' place was soundproof. If not, he hoped Venus kept Katya at the front of the plane in the forward family quarters.

Millie took out her phone and shot off a quick text as she slid her pants off. "Forward cabin has door." She was as breathless as he was, sucking in air through her nose, her nostrils flaring. "Not sure I can be quiet."

"Was just thinking the same thing," he growled. "Fuck! Help me get my pants off!"

Shadow needed her so bad he was shaking. How had he gone from comforting a child to nearly out of control so quickly? When Millie had mentioned the battle earlier, it was just like he'd come fresh from it. His heart rate picked up, sweat erupted over his skin, and a driving, burning need to fuck his precious Lyudmila until he found the oblivion he sought.

She'd been a virgin when he'd fucked her the

first time. He had no idea why she didn't tell him that, but it had been a defining moment for him. He'd known then he'd be the only man to have her, even if he had to beat the fuck outta some dumb shit for trying to move in on him. Which was why he needed to calm his ass down so he could be careful with her. He absolutely would not hurt her, no matter what he needed.

"I see that look on your face," she said as she sank to her knees, yanking down his pants and boxer briefs. "You think I can't handle what you need to give me." She bared her teeth as she grabbed his cock at the base in a tight fist. "You don't get to make that decision. I say when I'm ready. I say what I can take and when to stop."

"Millie --"

"No, Shadow!" She squeezed even tighter. "I say!" Then she slipped her lips over the head of his cock and drew him into her mouth. Then Shadow couldn't think anymore.

Chapter Eight

She absolutely wasn't letting Shadow hold back. Not now. She knew he needed free rein with her body, and that was exactly what she was going to give him. Sure, they could have fought, but the kind of fighting he needed involved him punching things. In a fight between them, even sparring, Millie could absolutely not let him punch her. Even if he pulled his punch, he'd likely hurt her. No. Shadow needed rough, pounding sex. Since she wasn't willing to let him have it with anyone else, Millie was what he had.

And when exactly had she decided she was keeping him? Because she absolutely was not giving him up without a fight. She would be what he needed, when he needed, because she wanted to keep him. Shadow was everything she wanted in a man. In the short time she'd known him -- hours, really -- she could see his character, his caring, and his responsible nature. He was protective and loving and everything missing in her life.

She'd missed seeing him the first time. Now, she was glad she had. Because no way would she let him near her with that thing if she had. He was long and thick. Intimidating. His cock was smooth, dark skin with thick veins and a large head, currently leaking precum out of the slit in the top. Eager to taste that precum, Millie stuffed as much of it as she could into her mouth, bobbing back and forth until Shadow threaded his fingers through her hair to control her movements the way he wanted to.

Instantly, he was more aggressive than she'd been. She wasn't used to it, but even though he needed more, he seemed to have a sixth sense about when to stop. His eyes were closed in bliss, yet he knew she needed to back off. It was the only reason she let him get away with not letting her orgasm. Because it was obvious he was lost in his own pleasure. That was all she wanted.

Millie continued to suck him for long minutes. Saliva occasionally dripped down her chin to her chest, and she didn't try to keep herself clean. She wanted this. Messy. Sweaty. She wanted it all. More importantly, she knew Shadow needed it even more than she did.

Finally, when he'd had enough, he pulled her to her feet by her hair. He shoved her to the bed, pressing her back to the mattress when she would have sat up to watch him. Unlike last time, Shadow was able to spread her legs wide, opening her up to him so her pussy was as exposed as it could be. Shadow wasted no time. He lowered his face and took a long swipe of her pussy from opening to clit.

"I'll never be able to get enough of your taste, Millie," he rasped out. "Nothin' sweeter."

"Do it again," she moaned. "Please."

He did, but his slow and gentle strokes soon became more and more frantic. His growls were loud in the small cabin. Soon he was eating her ferociously, shaking his head as he latched onto her clit. Then he bit down on her pussy lips, stretching them as he looked up her body to meet her gaze. Nothing had ever looked so animalistic as Shadow in that moment. His eyes seemed to gleam with the predator he hid deep inside him, the animal inside him finally slipping its leash.

"Gettin' ready to fuck you hard, woman. Gonna fuck you hard. You ready?"

"Yes," she gasped out. "I need you inside me!"

He lay between her thighs, his cock a pulsing

thing between them. Then he shifted his hips and guided the tip to her entrance, sinking inside her with a smooth, long stroke. Lyudmila gasped but arched into him. He stretched her, filled her full of his cock.

Again, he gave her time to adjust, his fingers tangling in her hair once more as he found her mouth with his. He kissed her over and over, dipping his tongue inside to tangle with hers. He didn't coax. He wasn't gentle, exactly -- he demanded she give him what he wanted, and she did, willingly.

"You feel so fuckin' good. Hot little pussy."

"All for you, Shadow."

"Yeah." He sounded satisfied. Smug. "It is."

Without warning, he pulled out and flipped Millie over, shoving her farther onto the bed as he mounted her from behind. His big body towered over her smaller one. Shadow gripped her hips as he increased his pace. When he was riding her hard, pulling her body back to meet his thrusts, Millie snagged a pillow from the bed and buried her face in it to scream.

"*O Bozhe! Trakhni menya!*"

"Yeah," Shadow agreed. "I'm definitely gonna fuck you. Fuck!"

With each surge forward, with each slap of flesh on flesh, Shadow grunted louder and louder until finally, his cock swelled inside her. Then she felt his hot cum spurting inside her. Millie cried out again into the pillow. Shadow leaned over her, biting her shoulder and shuddering above her. Sweat coated their bodies, making them glide together in a sensual slide.

Shadow collapsed onto his side, taking Millie with him. He was still buried inside her, his cock still semi-hard.

"Fuuuuck," he groaned. "That was…"

"Yeah," she agreed, giving him a small laugh when all she wanted to do was close her eyes and go to sleep right there. "It definitely was." She couldn't, though. She had to know what had happened to him that he felt like he couldn't show his darker side. "Tell me what happened with your ex, Shadow. Not because I believe any of that shit you told me earlier. You'd never hurt a woman if you could avoid it. Even if she deserved it."

Shadow was still for so long, Millie thought he might have dozed off. Then he sighed. "Fuck, Millie."

"Hey," she said, turning so she faced him. "You can tell me. I'm not here to judge."

"Fine." He scrubbed a hand over his face, then began. "When I met Carrianne, I was only a couple years out of high school. Workin' for a company like ExFil in Mississippi. I lied to her. I told her I was part owner and that I only worked with the grunts to show them how things were done. I made enough money it was relatively easy to convince her I was more than I was. Until she got pregnant.

"I had to come clean and, believe me when I tell you, it wasn't easy. We fought. Not physically, but, man, that was one nasty-ass argument. And she was totally right to be angry. I mean, yeah, she'd had her IUD removed without telling me, then told me she wanted sex without anything between us. But I wasn't mad about that. At least, not at first. The more she yelled at me, the more angry I got. When I finally exploded, I was so loud and angry it was my neighbors who called the cops. Once they got involved, I could see the wheels turning in Carrianne's mind.

"She *sobbed*. Uncontrollably. Being in Mississippi, me being a huge Black man and her this cute little redhead, even without a mark on her, she convinced the officer I'd hit her." Millie could see the simmering rage in Shadow's eyes even talking about it.

"How long ago was this?"

He shrugged. "Ten… fifteen years?"

"Shadow."

"Fine. It's been thirteen years, ten months, and fourteen days."

"And your child?"

"Carrianne dangled custody in front of me like a carrot. Never offering full custody, not not offering it either. She didn't want my child any more than she wanted me. She only wanted me for the money she thought I had, so she used my son to try to get as much money out of me as she could. It worked too. I was willing to do anything for the boy, which she knew."

"Why do I get feeling something bad happened?"

"Cause you're fuckin' smart?" He scrubbed a hand over his face, reaching for Millie and pulling her on top of him. With a swift movement, he aimed his cock at her pussy and pushed her down on top of him. She gasped but just lay forward on top of him so she could kiss him.

"Tell me. We get this out now, Shadow."

"Derrick," he said, looking off to the side, not wanting her to see the emotion in his eyes.

"What?"

"Derrick Brown. My name."

"Oh. OK. My last name is Volkov. Venus's too. Katya's is Zaitsev. Do you want me to call you Derrick?"

"Nah. Left that name behind after…" He gave her a small smile. "After." Taking a breath, he continued. "Just thought you should know what my name was since you ain't leavin' me."

She smiled. "Just so. Now. Continue."

"Anyway, after the baby was born, we went through the usual court battle. I wanted visitation at the very least. With the domestic violence charge against me, and having drawn a judge who wasn't overly sympathetic to fathers in general but Black fathers in particular, all I was able to get was supervised visits once a month, provided it didn't inconvenience Carrianne."

"Wow. Harsh."

"Yeah. Oh. And a hefty child support payment. I honestly didn't mind that. If nothing else, I figured I owed Carrianne because I'd lied to her in the first place. Because, I had to face it, there was no way that woman slept with me unless there was money involved for her. Ain't sayin' she was a whore. She was looking to cash in on the rich mercenary who was gone all the time."

"I see. Kind of like having your cake and eating it too?"

"Exactly like that. She got my money, but, since I was gone more months than I was home, she could have all the men she wanted, and I'd never be the wiser. Or to be able to blame her, really. While some of the men I served with had faithful spouses, a couple of them had an arrangement where, if they were gone more than a couple of weeks, their spouses were free to hook up as long as they used protection against pregnancy." He shrugged. "I could respect that, even if I didn't want it for myself."

"So what happened next?"

"I took my visitation every chance I could get. As my son got older, he got to be too much trouble for Carrianne. Her parents kept him most of the time. Believe it or not, they sympathized with me. Probably because I kept up with my child support payments and called every week to check on him. By the time he was five, Facetime was in use. Trey was with Carrianne's parents most of the time, so I bought them a cell phone specifically for Facetime with Trey. I called almost every day.

"I think that, because I did this, they saw how much Trey meant to me. Saw that, not only did I want to be in his life, I was trying my best to be a good father. They invited me to their house at least once a week when they knew Carrianne wouldn't be there so I could spend time with Trey without her drama."

"Sounds like you won over her parents."

"I guess I did. Which kind of surprised me. Her father tried to kill me right after he found out she was pregnant. I'd only met the man once in the six months we dated, and he hadn't been impressed."

"Wait. He tried to kill you?"

"Well, yeah." Shadow said this matter-of-factly. Like he fully expected it from the beginning. "I was a roughneck mercenary, not to mention a Black man in the deep South. Her daddy was livid with both of us. Since he couldn't very well stay mad at his daughter, he took out his anger and aggression on me." He shrugged like it was really no big deal.

"That's so wrong! Can't you see how wrong that is?"

"Of course, I can, sugar. But, from a male perspective, had she been my daughter, I'd have been livid too. Probably would have killed the bastard and never looked back. Not because of race or anything like that. Because the fucker had hit my daughter. Remember, I'd been charged. At the time, I hadn't been to court but the charges were there, and Carrianne told everyone who would listen how I'd hit her. I wasn't as big then as I am now, but I was still twice her size. Naturally, her daddy would believe her. And it was my neighbors who called the cops."

"I see. I suppose when you look at it that way." She cocked her head to the side. "How can you be so patient with something like that? You sound as if it's all a matter of course."

He shrugged. "Not sure. It angered me at the time. But I was man enough to admit I wasn't completely innocent. I'd yelled at her. OK, so I'd roared at her. I'd smashed a lamp and turned over a table, but I never touched her. I still let my temper get the best of me, so I could see how it would have scared her. Did I deserve her to tell everyone I'd laid hands on her? No. But I wasn't blameless. Hell, I'd have left my dumb ass too. I'm a big guy. If I have an explosion of temper, anyone in their right mind is gonna be frightened. Whether or not I get physical. That's a fact."

"So, her parents began to see you as a father. Not an enemy."

"Oh, absolutely. Her daddy even apologized for having pulled a gun on me that first meeting we had after Carrianne's accusations. He also said I deserved more than just visitations. I deserved joint custody if I wanted it. That was the last time I was in their house. The last day I saw my son alive."

"Fuck, Shadow," she whispered, kissing his neck and jaw before finding his lips for a tender kiss once more. It was for comfort, and she was sure he took what she was offering. Their lips lingered together for a few seconds before she pulled back, stroking his jaw with her fingers.

"Yeah. Carrianne either came to pick up Trey early, which wasn't likely, or she just happened to drive by and see my car.

"I never figured out how she ended up back at the house. We were out back, passing a football when she stormed outside, yelling at me and her parents. She was drunk and high, in no condition to drive. Trey was seven at the time. He'd already decided he wanted to be with me or his grandparents. Carrianne could be a handful, and it was painfully obvious she wanted little to do with Trey. But, having figured out her parents were letting me have time with him, and learning her dad was going to help me get joint custody, she snagged Trey by the arm and dragged him to her car, vowing none of us would ever see him again.

"We all tried to stop her, but she was quick on her cell to 911. She'd called and tearfully described a scene where I'd stormed into her parents' house and was beating Trey and the elderly couple. Everyone was yelling at her to put the phone down, to let Trey go. I'm sure the 911 operator heard nothing but absolute chaos, which was exactly the scene she described.

"She managed to shove Trey into her car and sped off. Her dad followed up with a 911 call of his own, telling them what had actually happened, and that she was obviously under the influence of something, driving at a high rate of speed with a child in the car."

The shuddering breath Shadow took nearly broke Millie's heart. It was obvious where this was going, and she wasn't sure she could listen to the rest. But she knew Shadow was reliving it because she'd insisted on hearing it. So she kissed him once more. Courage for both of them.

"I never found out what happened exactly, but there was a high-speed chase with the police. There were differing accounts, and I didn't really care because the end result was that she hit the railing of a bridge so hard, the car flipped over the top and into the river below. Neither of them survived. I went a little crazy then. Had it not been for my brothers, I have no idea what would have happened to me. I threw myself into work. And therapy, believe it or not. I wanted control of my temper. In my mind, it was that loss of control that started this whole thing in the first place. Like a death spiral that never should have happened. It worked. I also learned it was something I would always have to work on. The demon would always be there, waiting to get free. So when it gets too close, I work out. Or fight in a controlled environment."

"Or have wild, raunchy sex?" She gave him a lopsided grin, trying to take the sting out of it, but understanding the emotions he had to set free.

He grinned at her. "Yeah. Sometimes. Doesn't happen often. In fact, this is the first time in a very long time I've felt that pull. All because I was afraid I was gonna lose you, Millie." He shook his head. "I can't lose you."

"You realize this has been so fast as to not even be believed. Right? Literally *hours*, Shadow. Are you sure about this?"

"Honey, I was sure about us the moment I laid eyes on you. You were fierce, explosive dynamite in the tiniest package I'd ever seen. And yeah. You could kick my ass because you have no concept of fair fighting, and there would be no way I could ever hurt you. Hell, not even sure I could beat you if I didn't care to hurt you. You're that good."

She gave a little snort. "Of course, I'm that good. I tried to tell you, but you didn't want to listen."

He pulled her closer and wrapped his arms even

tighter around her. "The perfect woman for me." His cock pulsed inside Millie, and he gave a little thrust before rolling them over, his arms still securely around her. "You're fuckin' amazing."

Then he kissed her as he moved in long, slow strokes. Millie's breath caught, her legs falling wide as she surrendered to Shadow. He was vigorous, but only in the most delicious way. Even though she was sore, he still gave her so much pleasure it was difficult to believe. When she came this time, Shadow's mouth was firmly on hers, swallowing her screams. She did the same for him.

When it was over, they were both panting, sweat coating their skin.

"I love you, Millie," he said gruffly. "Ain't never felt like this about anyone but my parents and my brothers. Even then it was different. What I feel for you is… beyond compare."

"I love you, too. Only people who even come close in my life are Venus and Katya, and Venus and I have a lot to work out. But *da*. Is different."

"Can't promise you happy ever after, but I can promise to get as close to it as I can. And I'll never leave you, Lyudmila. I'd never have taken you without protection if I hadn't planned on keeping you. You're mine. I'm yours. I'll always be faithful to you."

She smiled and kissed him gently. "I promise the same, Derrick. I'm yours. You're mine. I should chastise you for not using a condom, but I can't. I'll love any child we conceive together. I'll protect him or her with my life."

"I know, sugar. I know."

Shadow got up and retrieved a wet cloth to clean her with, then himself before crawling back in bed with her. He pulled her close, wrapping his arms around her again in a warm cocoon. "Sleep now. When we get to Somerset, we can settle in for a while."

"Somerset. Yeah. why aren't we going back to Palm Springs?" She didn't really care. She'd go wherever Shadow wanted to go.

"Because it was easier for Cain. Besides, Bones is my home club, and they should be the first to meet my woman and her little sister."

"Venus might have reservations about that. Does she know?"

"Yeah. She was surprisingly agreeable." He chuckled. "I think there's a brother there she has her eyes on, but I have no idea who."

"Well, we'll just have to figure it out and set them up."

"My thoughts exactly. Woman needs a man who curbs this fetish she has with pink."

Millie barked out a laugh before burying her face in his shoulder and dissolving into a fit of giggles. Shadow's warm laugh vibrated through her, and Millie knew she was home. Forever home. Her and Shadow. As long as they were together, she knew they could do anything. She felt it in her soul.

With that thought foremost in her mind, happier than she could ever remember being, Millie drifted off to sleep. Safe in the arms of the only man she'd ever loved.

Carnage Bones (MC 11)
A Bones MC Romance
Marteeka Karland

Calliope: I've made some bad choices, but this time I was about to make the biggest mistake of my life -- all because another mistake had come back to haunt me, putting my adopted sons at risk. In sheer desperation I turned to some bikers on the road for help. One in particular -- the man they call Carnage -- seems to wrap his mantle of protection around us. What I didn't know is, his club is home to the twins' father. Once again, I know I'll have to pay the consequences for my bad decisions. What can I do if he decides he wants custody of his sons? I'm not sure even Carnage can save us this time.

Carnage: I really do try to steer clear of trouble, but when a frightened woman with two kids flags us down on the road, I can't leave them to face their fate alone. I know I'm bringing trouble home with us, all the way back to Kentucky and the very heart of my club. One thing's for sure -- I have questions that need answers. I promised Calliope I'll never let anyone separate her from her boys, and I mean to stand by that promise. There's no way I'm letting anyone take what's mine. Carnage isn't just a name. It's what follows in my wake when people get in my way.

Chapter One
Carnage

There's nothing quite as satisfying as flying down a long stretch of highway on my bike. I enjoyed the feeling as much as I could during the run I was currently leading my club, Bones MC, on, coming back from Palm Beach, Florida to Somerset, Kentucky. I had to be focused, but it didn't keep me from enjoying life.

Bones had a group of twelve bikers on this run. At least half had ol' ladies with us, which was a fight. I don't like women riding this long with us. The run was close to sixteen hours, which we'd had to break down into two legs. I'd have preferred three, but Cain had given me the stink eye. Anyone other than Cain, and I'd have told them to suck it up. Surprisingly, the women complained about having to stop more often than not. They'd turned out to be stouter than I'd given them credit for. I still insisted on stopping every three hours, though, even if it was only ten minutes or so.

The trip had been wonderful for everyone, and the ride completely uneventful. I'd mapped out the route to keep out of other club's territory and had made sure to stick to the main traffic thoroughfares when entering a county where local law enforcement wasn't exactly friendly to MCs. Everything had gone smoothly. Until the last two hours.

No matter what route we took, no matter how slow or fast I led the run, there was a small Ford Fusion tailing us. I'd nearly missed it behind Tool's bigass chase vehicle. The mechanic had a massive Ford F350 with a gooseneck trailer that carried everything we could need if anyone broke down. But the Ford was there. Blue. Driving safely, but still tailing us.

It was time to make everyone aware. Well,

everyone other than the ol' ladies. No reason to worry the women.

I keyed the mic on my helmet's headset. "I need everyone's attention," I said. "Tool. You got a blue Fusion on your six."

"Yeah. Picked it up after the last stop. Think there's a girl drivin'. Male passenger. Not sure but I think there's kids in the back."

"So, harmless?" Sword didn't sound convinced. I wasn't sure he was wrong. Something was definitely pinging my radar.

"Tool, they made any move like they wanted to pass?"

"Hard to say, Carnage. I get the feeling the guy wants the girl to go around, but she's refusing. They argue when he's awake. Not sure if that's the reason or not. She meets my gaze in the mirror when I slow down, though. Looks more than a little stressed."

"Well, *that's* not a red flag or anything," Bohannon muttered.

Bohannon was the enforcer of Bones while Sword was his backup. I always welcomed advice from the enforcers, but final say on anything during a run fell to me. The road captain. Cain was the president of Bones MC. Torpedo the vice president. Though both had a say, they would defer to me on a run because I had the plan. I knew the layout of the land and had chosen the route specifically with all aspects of their surroundings in mind.

"She tryin' to communicate with you in any way?" Cain asked. "Not that she reasonably could."

"No…" Tool trailed off, but offered nothing else. "She turned on her blinker a time or two, but didn't make a move to pull off the interstate."

"Maybe she wants us to make a stop?" That from

Bohannon.

I thought for a minute. "Yeah. It's time anyway. We'll pull off at exit eighty-seven. There should be a minimart with gas just off the exit on the right. That's two miles down the road. See if you can get her to understand that."

"And if it's an ambush?"

Bohannon had a valid point, but I didn't think so. "Then be ready to defend yourselves against however many can reasonably fit inside a fucking small-ass Fusion."

It was a moment before we passed the sign that had the symbols for the main interests at the exit, then Tool came back on the radio. "I gave three separate right turn signals, and she flashed her brights at me. The man in the car appears to be asleep."

"Copy that," I acknowledged. "Everyone, prepare for a stop. We'll let her make the first move."

* * *

Calliope

My heart pounded. I glanced back at the boys, hoping they knew to stay quiet. My boyfriend, Mark, was asleep in the passenger seat, thankfully. He hadn't wanted to make any stops, but not taking a break every few hours wasn't an option with twin eight-year-olds in the car. The boys looked at me but didn't make a sound. Just one more reason I knew I was doing the right thing.

As the group of motorcycles pulled off the exit, I followed, hoping and praying Mark would stay asleep until I had the boys safely out of the car. He was less likely to get violent in front of people than he was at home. Or wherever it was he was taking us. What I was getting ready to do was a huge risk, but staying in my current situation with Mark was going to have a deadly outcome. I might not know these guys personally, but I was in a hell of a mess.

The boys' father, my sister's boyfriend, had been a member of an MC in Indiana. The only piece of advice he'd given us before leaving had been not to judge motorcycle clubs just because they were MCs. It had been part of the reason he'd given my sister for not sticking around. She was too judgy. I knew I'd been just as judgy as my sister, and I didn't blame Chase for leaving. For all his perceived faults, and even though he'd left her, I still couldn't reconcile the Chase I'd known with him leaving Cherry pregnant and on her own. Chase had always seemed to revere family. Had talked about wanting a family of his own.

This club's name was Bones and hailed from Kentucky, according to the patches the members were wearing on their vests. That was heading in the direction Mark wanted me to go, but perhaps this group could help me and the boys get to safety.

I moved behind the group at a store just off the exit ramp and pulled up to the gas pump, away from the bikers. I'd put my debit card in my back pocket several miles back, hoping I'd have the opportunity to take the boys and slip off. It would leave Mark with the car, but it was a small price to pay. As if sensing what needed to happen, both boys had their seatbelts off and were out of their booster seats with their backpacks ready. Theodore sat behind me, so he was ready. Sebastian, careful not to bump Mark's seat, moved to stand beside his brother, ready to exit the vehicle the second I opened the door. I left the engine running in the hopes Mark would continue to sleep.

I snagged my wallet. It had everything but my credit card, which Mark had confiscated a few weeks ago to carry with him for "emergencies." Then, as quietly as I could, I got out of the car. Without a word, the boys grabbed their backpacks and hopped out when I opened the door.

"Where you goin'?" Mark opened his eyes sleepily and gave me an angry stare. He was high and drunk, and his speech was slurred markedly. He'd passed the manic stage an hour ago and usually slept several hours afterward.

"The boys and I both need a bathroom break, and I thought I'd top off the tank."

He looked at them, his eyelids drooping. "Well, be quick 'bout it. No more stops till we get to 'Tucky."

I took a breath and shut the door, then swiped my card through the reader, selecting the cheapest grade of gas before putting the nozzle in the gas tank and clicking it on the slowest fill rate it had. With any luck, Mark would sleep for a long time. It was possible no one would notice until I was safely away. If not? Well. I'd figure it out.

Taking the boy's hands, I walked toward the store, glancing over at the bikers. None of them seemed to pay me any attention but the one from the truck I'd been following. Another one walked toward the store. He had his eyes on me like he was on a mission. His cold, hard look gave me a frisson of apprehension, but I was committed now. I went straight to the bathroom area in case Mark followed us inside, then stood waiting in the narrow hallway.

It wasn't long before one of the men approached me. He was tall with a full, reddish-brown beard and was covered in tattoos. His hair was a lighter mix of red and brown. He sported dreadlocks on top of his head, grown long and tied back in a tail. The sides of his head were shaven, leaving only stubble to obscure a few tats creeping up his neck into his hair and over his forehead and cheek. Fine scars crisscrossed his forehead and cheeks. I assumed his beard hid several too, but it was hard to tell. And the man was hella big. Tall and muscular, he looked so scary I worried I'd made a serious mistake.

The boys stood their ground, lifting their chins. Theodore moved slightly in front of me while Sebastian dropped his backpack on the floor as if readying for a fight. Both twisted out of my grip on their hands.

The big man glanced at them and seemed to read the situation. "You in trouble?"

"Mark's takin' us to Kentucky," Sebastian said. "I don't wanna go to Kentucky, and neither does Theo."

"Mark the man in the car with you?"

"Yeah," Sebastian confirmed. Theo just stared at the man as if sizing him up. An eight-year-old. Trying to figure out how to take down a full-grown man this guy's size. It made me want to grind my teeth in frustration and cry all at the same time. Kids the boys' age shouldn't be worried about how to protect themselves or their mom.

"He your dad?" The guy didn't acknowledge me. Just talked to the boys.

When I put my arm around Sebastian's shoulder, he shrugged me off and stepped closer to his brother. Not as if for protection, but like his brother was the better fighter and he had Theo's back. It was ridiculous, really. The kids were *eight*! "Mark? No way! He's an asshole."

I gasped. "Sebastian!"

Bastian looked over his shoulder at me. "Well, he is." Then he turned back to the biker. "He hits Mommy. Tried to hit Theo too, but I hit him with a baseball bat."

Now the biker focused on me, looking me up and down. He paused on the bruise across my cheek, but continued to take in everything. I had bruises on my legs that I knew were visible where my shorts stopped mid-thigh and a few on my arms where my T-shirt didn't cover them. This guy seemed to take in every single one of them. As he did, his frown deepened until he looked positively livid. The boys saw it too. Instead of being afraid, however, Theo nodded at the guy.

"Yeah," Sebastian said, as if the guy had actually voiced his anger. "We got mad too. Mark's out in the car if you want to go hit him back. I ain't strong enough. I hit him with the bat, but it didn't hurt him."

Again, the biker looked at me. His green eyes were so intense I shivered. "You want out?"

I glanced at the boys. "I'm afraid…" I swallowed. "The boys…"

He nodded. "Come with me. Tool and I will escort you to the truck."

"Tool?" Sebastian said, looking incredulous. "Ain't bikers supposed to have cool names? What kinda name is Tool?"

Another large man approached them. He glanced around the store as if looking for threats. When he got closer, he glanced at the other guy, then smiled at the boys. "You guys need a lift?"

"Why you called Tool?" Sebastian asked instead of answering the question.

Tool shrugged. "'Cause I'm good with all kinds of tools." He grinned. "I fix stuff."

"Oh. Well, I guess it's OK. Still kinda dumb, though."

"Sebastian, please," I all but pleaded. "If these

men can help us, you don't need to insult them."

"So, if they don't wanna help I can insult them, then?"

"No. Boys, please. Just… get back here and let me handle this." I knew I was doing a piss-poor job of things so far, but I was so scared I was quaking in my shoes. The boys didn't seem to have any fear. I supposed after living with Mark for the past few months they weren't afraid of anything. That was on me.

"Take the kids to the truck. I'll have a talk with their mother."

"No!" OK, things were starting to get real. All the ways this could go badly were starting to make themselves known. "They don't leave me." I grabbed the backs of the boys' shirts and pulled them to me. Thankfully, they didn't resist, but they didn't seem scared either.

"Take it easy, girl. We ain't gonna hurt your kids. I need some answers, and I'm pretty sure you don't want to talk about this in front of your boys."

"Can't it wait until after we get out of here?"

He seemed to think about that for a moment, then spoke to Tool. "Put the boys in the truck. I'll bring their mama and drive." He glanced around. "Change of plan. I'm driving the cage. Tool's road captain."

Tool looked at him and nodded. "Come on, boys. Sounds like the guy in the car might be wakin' up."

Before I could stop them, the boys snagged their backpacks and headed through the store with Tool.

"Oh no," I whispered. My gaze clung to the big biker's. "He'll never let us go willingly." I turned to the big one. "Look. The boys. They're my sister's kids. She died from cervical cancer right after they were born. I adopted them. They call me Mama, but I'm not really.

Mark knows that. He also claims to know their father, and he threatened to take them away if we left."

"Why does he want you with him so bad?" The guy was gruff, and there was a temper on this one, but he seemed to have an iron control over it.

"Because of my sister's insurance money. But, honestly, he went through the last of it a few weeks ago. He just doesn't believe me."

"What was it finally made you take the risk?"

I shivered. "When Sebastian hit him with the bat. Theo actually brought out a gun, going to kill him. Theo said the only reason he didn't shoot was because he was afraid he'd accidentally hit me." I shook my head. "I don't want them to have to kill to protect me. I should have left before it got that bad, but I have no idea if Mark was telling the truth about knowing Chase. And that was the first time he'd ever gotten physical with the boys. Before, it was only me."

"You're right. You shoulda left long before it came to that. As to Mark, you leave him to us. Come on." He grabbed my upper arm and started to lead me away, then stopped. "You and the kids need something to eat or drink?"

"I -- the boys might."

"They do juices or soda?"

"Milk," she said. "They like milk. Usually, they'll get some pretzels or peanuts. Occasionally a cupcake or Twinkie."

"OK, then."

He headed to the refrigerated section, and I got chocolate for Sebastian, white for Theodore. Then I snagged some pretzels and peanuts. The guy grabbed several more snacks along with another bottle of white and chocolate milk and some sodas. He plopped them all down on the counter, and the cashier rang them up and bagged them.

I pulled out my card to pay but the guy stopped me. "My run. I pay."

"I can --"

"I pay."

He gave the guy cash, then snagged the bag and my arm again. When they got outside, I could see Mark was indeed awake. He staggered around the car, yelling about how the "dumb bitsch can do nuttin' righ'." He fell to one knee before righting himself. Then fell again.

"Oh, God," I whimpered. "If he sees us…"

"He won't. Come on." He opened the door to the big truck and helped me in. The boys were already strapped into their booster seats.

"Cain and Sword got the seats while the guy was sleeping. Probably what woke him up, but he's not missed anything yet," Tool said to me.

"Good. Let's get the fuck outta here."

"On it."

"Follow the route. We're four hours from home. No stopping unless it's an emergency."

"I'll keep everyone safe," Tool said, then winked at the boys. "You guys behave. Your mama don't, Carnage will help you spank her."

"Oh, boy!" Sebastian's face lit up. "I finally get to spank Mommy!"

"Oh?" Tool raised an eyebrow. "She have to spank you a lot?"

"Nah. But she says she's gonna."

Theodore looked at the big man getting into the truck. "Your name's Carnage?"

"Yeah. They say it's because I cause trouble wherever I go."

"I'm trouble, too," Theo said. "Mark hates me

'cause I don't let him steal stuff in stores."

Carnage flicked a glance at me, and I ducked. "I see. Good job keeping him honest."

"He ain't honest," Theo said. He looked disgruntled as he turned to look out the window. "He's mean, and I hate him."

"You're not supposed to hate anybody," I said automatically. I glanced up at the big biker -- Carnage -- then ducked down again.

"He hates us. So I hate him." Theodore didn't raise his voice or anything. Just looked out the truck window to where the car was parked. Mark was still struggling to get back into the passenger's seat. He called out for me several times, shortening my name to Callie. Theo got a fierce look on his face before flipping the man off through the window. "Most of all," Theodore turned back to Carnage, "he's gonna hurt Mommy if we let him."

"Boy," Carnage said, obviously having had enough, "if you believe nothing else any of us tell you, believe me when I say that man will *never* hurt your mother again. Or either of you."

"He was gonna," Sebastian said, his eyes wide. "When he got us to Kentucky. Me and Theo heard 'im say he was gonna get rid of that bitch's little brats. I'm pretty sure he meant us."

"Oh no," I gasped. "Oh, God."

Carnage turned around and started the truck. "I gotcha, kid. We're headed to Kentucky, but back to the Bones compound. You'll be safe there while we sort everything out."

"No, we won't," Theo said softly. "He's got buddies gonna come after us. Said some of 'em were in motorcycle gangs, too." Theo looked Carnage straight in the eye before he said, "Probably you guys. You're from Kentucky. Right?"

"You give me some time, boy, I'll take care of this for y'all. And no. We ain't the kinda club that hurts women and children."

I couldn't say anything. I just stared in horror as Mark finally slumped back into the passenger's seat of my car, the door open as he passed out once again. I'd been taking my kids possibly to their deaths, and I had gone along with that monster.

"You good?" Carnage reached across the console and gripped my shoulder gently.

"Not sure I'll ever be good again." Tears dripped down my cheeks, but I held back any other noise so I didn't distress my sons.

"Hold it together. I know you can."

I nodded. "I can." I sniffed and rubbed my arm over my eyes. "I will."

Chapter Two
Carnage

The next four hours passed with no incidents. The woman -- Callie, the asshole back there had called her -- occasionally cried silently while Theodore brooded, looking out the window. Probably trying to figure out as many ways as he could to take me out. I respected the kid. He wasn't arguing with anyone, just rolling with the situation and adapting.

Sebastian talked almost nonstop. Normally I would have scowled and told the little shit to shut up, but the kid was awesome. Fierce like his brother, he'd still retained some of that kid personality all young children had. Theodore talked sometimes, but he was more reserved and introspective. I was certain he was still thinking about that Mark character along with wondering what this new situation called for.

Callie hadn't said much, but I thought I could get her talking once we got to Somerset. God, she was wreaking havoc on my senses! Not only did I want to coax her out of her funk, but I wanted to coax her into my bed. See how far I could go with her. She was so fragile, but I got the feeling there was more to her than what was on the surface. She was beaten down. A victim when she was doing her best to be a good mother to her boys. I wanted to get her to play. With me. But first, I wanted to make her forget all her worries and lean on me. I wanted to wrap her in bubble wrap and show her that not all men were assholes.

Right now, though, keeping up with Sebastian was proving a struggle. The kid asked more questions than any ten people I'd ever been around. I found myself grinning at the endless stream, though, instead of being irritated. And I had no idea why.

"Hey, Carnage." And, yeah. The kid started every question with, "Hey, Carnage."

"Yeah, kid?" It was the standard response from me.

"How'd you get those scars?"

Callie gasped. "Sebastian!"

Ignoring her, I shrugged. "In battle," I said proudly. "Don't get close-up fighting much these days, but I was in a fight a few years ago that got up close and personal."

"Did you give the other guy scars?" Sebastian's eyes were wide and almost maniacal. Most boys loved these sorts of tales, but I got the feeling these kids would more than most. Mainly because they'd been so powerless in their own fight with their mom's boyfriend.

"Sure did." The guy had died, but, yeah. I'd marked him as good as he'd marked me.

"Did you kill him?" That question was from Theodore. It was asked matter-of-factly, like it didn't mean that much if I didn't answer, but I knew it did.

I sighed. "Yeah, kid. I killed the bastard. He was holdin' a bunch of kids hostage. I couldn't blow the place up, so I went in, found the little shit, and taught him a lesson."

Theodore gave me a succinct nod, like he approved of my actions. For some fucking reason, my chest swelled with pride at the kid's approval. What the fuck? Since when did I need the approval of an eight-year-old?

"Hey, Carnage." And there went Sebastian again. I grinned.

"Yeah, kid?"

"Why'd you put dreadlocks in your hair?"

I shrugged. "'Cause it looks cool."

He laughed. "Yeah. Can I do my hair like that, Mommy?"

"We'll see," she said, softly. I could tell she was on the verge of another bout of crying. I hated it for her, but there was really nothing I could do about it right now. Later I'd figure something out.

"Hey, Carnage."

"Yeah, kid?"

"Are we there yet?"

I coughed to smother a laugh. That had been the only question the kid hadn't asked until now. Shoulda known it was coming. "Not much longer,"

"You gettin' sick? 'Cause if you're gettin' sick, you should take some medicine." No way anyone couldn't fall in love with Sebastian. If his mama and brother had been in a better frame of mind, I could happily see us barreling down the highway singing "Ninety-Nine Bottles of Beer on the Wall" at the top of our lungs after a long vacation.

"Nah, I ain't gettin' sick, Sebastian. You hungry? There's a few more snacks, I think." I raised the bag of snacks that were left.

"Only the unhealthy kind." Sebastian actually wrinkled his nose. "Mom doesn't like us eatin' unhealthy snacks."

"I think this one time it will be fine." Callie hadn't said much, but she encouraged snack time. "There's still some more chocolate milk if you want it."

"Sure!" The boy took the milk and the Twinkies and tore into both.

"Theodore?" Callie seemed to have pulled herself together, but her hold was tenuous at best, I thought.

"Nah, Mama. I'm good. You should eat, though.

You haven't eaten since breakfast and not much then." Theo met my gaze in the rearview mirror. "Asshole grabbed her biscuit and threw it out the window 'cause he said she was gettin' fat." Kid wrinkled his nose. "She gets sick to her stomach if she don't eat."

I wanted to turn around, go back to that fucking convenience store, and pound the fuck outa that Mark character. No kid should have such a weight on his shoulders. And Callie was too thin as it was. During that four-hour ride back to the Bones compound, I made up my mind I would make those boys act like eight-year-olds if it fucking killed me. Well, when I had a moment to think on it. Sebastian kept me running in circles with endless questions.

And I'd make their mother smile.

I glanced her way. Though she still silently wept occasionally, she held herself together. Just like I told her. When she seemed on the verge of losing it, she'd glance at me, and I'd reach over to squeeze her shoulder. That seemed to steady her.

God, she seemed so lost and broken. When the sunshine hit her face, the bruises stood out starkly. Thank God her face wasn't swollen, because I wasn't sure I could handle that. The bruises looked to be three- or four-days-old, still purple, but fading to a greenish yellow. This girl and her feisty boys brought out my protective instincts like nothing else had in years. I wanted to pound that little fuck into the Goddamned ground for doing this to her. The boys, though taking the whole thing seriously, seemed in a little better shape, but that was likely because they were kids. They didn't know any differently.

Despite the marks of violence on her face, Callie was strikingly lovely. She looked younger than she had to be given she'd raised the boys from birth, but she wasn't a kid. Just the haunted look in her eyes told me that much. She was slight of stature -- too skinny for my liking, but I suspected that had a lot to do with her living situation. Stress and likely lack of finances if her boyfriend had taken everything. Her hair was a light brown, cut short. Looked like she might have just hacked it off as it started bothering her, but she managed to pull the look off in a cute kind of way. She had a heart-shaped face and the cutest little button nose. Kind of reminded me of a fairy or something. A real-life Tinkerbell.

"We're almost to Somerset," I said softly when she caught my gaze again. "When we get there, Cain will have some questions for you. It will help you more if your answers are complete and truthful."

"Who's Cain?" She asked the question like it was expected of her, not because she really wanted the answer.

"Our president. I'm hoping we can get a handle on who the boys' father is and where he's located. We can shore up your legal claim from there once we know exactly who and what we're fighting."

She gasped. "You're not gonna call him, are you? Because I have no idea what he'd do. Cherry said she told him she was pregnant after she left, but I have no idea how that conversation went. All I know is that he never came back. But if she lied…"

"You think she'd do that? Lie about telling him about the boys?"

She shrugged. "I never thought so. But Chase always talked about wanting a family. The more I thought about it over the years, the more I wondered why he didn't at least come see the boys if he knew Cherry was pregnant."

"Did you try to contact him after she passed?"

"No. I didn't want to know," she admitted. "I wanted to take Cherry at her word because I loved them so much and they were all I had left of my sister. My only family."

I took a quick glance in the rearview, checking to see how closely the boys were listening before I continued. "We'd never set in motion anything to take the boys away from you. Even if they were in immediate danger. We'd simply remove them and you from the situation and reevaluate. We ain't social services."

"What if Chase wants them?"

"You adopted them?"

"Yes. Right after Cherry passed. In fact, she had it all fixed before then, making me their mother at the moment of their birth. She said she had her lawyer try to find Chase, but I wasn't involved in that. I was too busy trying to take care of Cherry."

"Fair enough. Do you know Chase's last name?"

"Yeah. It's Dutton. He was living in Indiana when they met, but worked for some paramilitary thing. They did protection detail or something. He was very secretive about it."

Carnage's gaze snapped to hers. "Chase Dutton. You're sure."

"Oh, God." She covered her mouth with her hand. "You know him."

"Just calm down, girl. Take a breath."

"We ain't goin' with no one other than Mama," Theodore said quietly. "I'll kill him if I have to, but I'm not leavin' my mama on her own."

"No one said you were, Theo," I assured him. "Just that I might know your daddy. If I'm right, he'll do what Cain says in this matter, no matter what the fuck he wants."

"Stop the car," Callie said. She'd gone pale, and sweat broke out over her face.

I knew that look. I pulled onto the shoulder, radioing the situation quickly so my brothers would know what was going on. A couple of them slowed down and waited on the shoulder ahead of us. The second the truck stopped, Callie opened the door and stumbled out.

"Callie! Wait! The truck's too high --" I was certain she fell, because she crawled to the grass beyond the shoulder and heaved over and over.

"Her name's Calliope," Theodore snapped. "Only *he* ever called her Callie."

"Shit," I muttered, snagging a bottle of water and a box of tissues before getting out of the truck. There was a lot to be addressed here, but my first concern was making sure Callie was OK. *No, Calliope. Her name's Calliope*. She must not like it being shortened. At the very least, Theodore didn't like it. Making an enemy of her kids wasn't going to help me help her. "You guys stay here. I'm just gonna help your mama." He glanced at Theodore. "And I'll call her Calliope from now on unless she says it's OK." The boy didn't say anything, just turned his head to watch his mother.

"If she's sick, she should take some medicine!" Sebastian called out.

I hurried around the truck to kneel beside her while she emptied the contents of her stomach. She heaved and heaved, tears streaming down her face until there was nothing left in her stomach.

When it finally passed, Calliope sat back on her heels. I handed her the box of tissues, and she wiped her face and mouth. When I handed her the water, she mumbled, "Thanks," before taking a swig and rinsing out her mouth. Then she took a couple more sips.

After a couple of minutes, I rested a hand on her back. "You good?"

"Chase is gonna take the boys, isn't he?"

I thought about that a minute. There was no way I could promise her Chase wouldn't get custody. Especially if he knew nothing about them and hadn't been given the opportunity to refuse his rights. "Ain't gonna lie to you, girl. I have no idea. What I *can* promise is that no one will take them away from you if they don't wanna go. And I'm pretty sure they don't wanna go. If I'm right, and this guy is who I think he is, you'll all be OK. Cain has a huge influence over him, and Cain is as good a man as they come."

"I've made everything worse," she sobbed. "I can't lose them. I just can't!"

"You've trusted me this far, Calliope. Trust me a little further."

She sniffed, blowing her nose delicately. "Doesn't seem like I have much of a choice now. I left that option back at that stupid gas station. This is all my fault for taking up with Mark in the first place." Before I could reply, she added, "And I should have tried to talk to Chase myself. He was right. I had a thing against motorcycle clubs and never gave him a chance. Deep down, I knew he'd want the boys, and I just took Cherry's word for it."

"I assume Mark wasn't abusive when you first got with him?" I ignored the other for now because, honestly, this wasn't the time.

"No. That didn't start until later. And only with me. Never the boys."

"Probably because he knew you'd leave and take the money with you."

She nodded. "Should have anyway."

Then I asked the one question I knew I shouldn't.

"So, why didn't you?"

She shrugged and looked away. "I just wanted to be with someone. I was tired of being on my own."

I rubbed the center of my chest. My heart ached for this girl, and I had no idea why. Maybe it was just the whole situation. It had come at me out of nowhere. I hadn't had a chance to prepare for the emotional backlash. I prided myself on my control, but I didn't seem to have control over my emotions in this situation. The girl just... tugged at me. Given who I thought the kids' daddy was, there might be a reason Chase left before he found out about the kids. That would have been about the time Data and Zora found each other, and Chase was into some really bad shit at the time. Maybe that's why he'd abandoned them, though that didn't sound like Chase. I had to face the possibility that Calliope's sister never told Chase about her pregnancy.

Later. I'd figure it out later. Right now, I needed to get them back to the compound and get Data on this. And see if the Chase Dutton in Bones was the same Chase who'd run out on his pregnant girlfriend and left the kids' future in the wind.

I helped Callie to her feet. "Tell me one thing before we get back into the car." When she nodded, I continued. "How old were you when the boys were born?"

"Sixteen," she said softly.

"No." I shook his head, crossing his arms over his chest. "Not buying it. No way you get custody of two infants at that age even if you're emancipated."

She shrugged. "It's all a matter of public record," she said. "State of Tennessee. Cherry's dad is dead. Our mother passed away when I was twelve from cervical cancer. Cherry died from the same. My dad is in the wind. Even the court couldn't find him." She met my gaze boldly. Proudly. "I got my GED when I turned sixteen. My sister had to sign for me, and we had to get permission from the school, but I was nobody's kid. I was an orphan being raised by my sister. I missed a lot of school anyway because I was working, trying to help Cherry keep a roof over our heads. Chase helped while he was around, but he and Cherry fought all the time over his MC ties. She didn't like it, and he got tired of explaining that not all MCs were bad.

When he left, it was just me and Cherry. I picked up a second job. Then Cherry found out about her cancer. During the preliminary tests, she found out she was pregnant. So she started planning. Got a lawyer to help us. I'm not sure, but I think maybe she did sexual favors for him to help pay his bill. He was always very touchy-feely with her, and I know we didn't have money to give him. At any rate, the situation was, Cherry was going to die. The kids were going to need someone to take custody of them. I was the only living relative, and I was self-sufficient. The lawyer got the judge to emancipate me so I could take custody of the boys rather than all three of us going into foster care. I had my GED, but my sister, being four years older, had custody of me."

"OK. Maybe I was a little too quick to jump all over that. I'll reserve judgment until Data gets me the documents." I wanted to believe her. Didn't want to think she could deceive me, but this had to be looked into. Preferably before Chase found out about the situation. I would never keep a good man from his children, but I didn't want to take the boys away from the only person who'd been a constant in their lives. Sure, she'd made a mistake, but she was still really young. Too young to have raised eight-year-old twins. "You good to go? We're only thirty minutes or so from the clubhouse."

"Yeah," she said, making her way back to the truck.

"One more thing. I'm gonna need your full name."

She sighed. "So you can dig up some dirt on me."

"You know we have to. For our own security, not just to do with Chase."

"Calliope Mills. If you want my driver's license, it's in my wallet."

"I'd appreciate it." I helped her in, and she handed me her license before I went around to the other side.

Bohannon was one of the two who'd pulled onto the shoulder to wait for us, but he'd circled back and came up beside us now. "Everything good?"

"Yeah. She got overwhelmed. Look. I need you to get Data to run her record. Specifically, the situation around her emancipated minor status eight or nine years ago. She gave me some information, and I want to see if it's correct."

"You mean you want to see how much bullshit she's feeding you."

"Yeah. Something like that." I scrubbed a hand behind my neck. "She's gettin' under my skin, and I don't like it." I handed her license over to Bohannon, who snapped a picture of it with his phone.

Bohannon nodded. "Understood. Just be careful. Don't piss her off too much until you figure out how much is true. I'll send this image to Data so he can get to work."

"There's something else." I hesitated. This could

get tricky. "Has Chase come back from his ExFil mission yet?"

"Don't think so. Due back soon."

"Good. We may have a situation."

Bohannon raised an eyebrow. "I take it you'll fill me in as soon as we get back?"

"Yeah. It'll wait. We're close to home, and I don't want to take a chance that that son of a bitch got his wits together and followed us."

"Good. I'll get Data on this. Me and Viper will bring you in."

I bumped forearms with Bohannon before getting into the truck. Then we all took off, headed home.

* * *

Calliope

Carnage pulled the big truck into what he called a clubhouse or compound. It was definitely a compound, looking more like a hotel or something. The boys were excited. At least Bastian was. Theo's eyes widened, but he didn't say much. I could tell he wanted to explore.

Most of the bikes were already parked in a row outside a big garage. The men talked and laughed with each other. A few women hung around, leaning against the wall or on one of the men. It wasn't until we pulled around back that I noticed other children playing.

"Mommy! Can we go play?" Sebastian was practically bouncing up and down in excitement. Sebastian was my social butterfly, so it didn't surprise me he was ready to play. But when Theodore echoed him, pretending reluctance, I knew I needed to make this happen.

"Do you think it would be all right?" I asked Carnage.

"Absolutely. Come on. I'll introduce you boys." Carnage was out of the truck and had the backseat door opened just as Sebastian was about to throw it open himself. I climbed out and followed. Sebastian ran ahead while Theo followed more sedately.

"Gunnar!" Carnage waved to a boy a few years older than Sebastian and Theodore. He ran over with a smile, looking the boys over welcomingly.

"What's up?"

"These are my guests. Sebastian and Theodore," Carnage introduced. "Can you show them around? Make them welcome?"

"You guys stayin'?" Gunnar addressed Sebastian. Probably because he had a huge smile on his face and was obviously eager to join the group.

Sebastian shrugged. "I don't know. We just got here."

"They'll be stayin' a while," Carnage said. "At least a few days. Maybe longer."

"Cool! The girls kinda got me outnumbered," Gunnar said with a grin. "You guys can even up the score."

Gunnar and Sebastian took off, but Theo hung back. "You OK, Mom?"

"Yeah, baby. You go play."

"I'll be takin' your mom inside for a while, Theodore. I'll bring her back soon, but we all gotta talk for a bit. You good with that?"

The question surprised me. Carnage didn't seem like the kind of man who'd defer to anyone, let alone a boy.

Theo looked up at me, obviously needing my opinion. "We'll only be a minute. You'll be so busy getting to know everyone you probably won't even miss me."

As serious as any kid could, he said, "Yes, I will."

I opened my arms for him. Theo stepped into them immediately. He hugged me, but, like always, he was hugging me for my comfort. Not the other way around.

"I'll be right out here if you need me, Mom." He looked up at Carnage. "If you hurt her, I'll figure out a way to hurt you worse."

Carnage nodded. "I understand. I hurt her, there will be several men around her will help you hurt me worse. You go to anyone. Have Gunnar help you or take you to his dad. Anyone hurts you, your brother, or your mother. You hear me?"

Theo took his time, studying Carnage, then he nodded. "I'm watching you."

"Understood."

A fresh flood of tears threatened to overwhelm me, but I blinked them back. Carnage seemed to know I needed a minute because he just stood there, watching as the kids got to know each other and began to play. They had a soccer ball they were kicking around in a big, green yard. Not really playing soccer, just… playing.

After a few moments, he grunted, taking me gently by the shoulder and turning me toward the building. "Come on. This won't take long. I'll have you back out to your boys as quick as I can."

I followed Carnage as he took me to a room that looked like it was someone's office. Inside was the one they called Cain and several others.

"Calliope Mills," Cain said. "This is my wife, Angel."

The other woman stepped forward. She looked

to be in her early thirties and very beautiful. "Hi, Calliope. I'm so happy to meet you." She reached out and took Calliope's hand and gripped it firmly. "I saw your boys go off with Gunnar. He's our son. Adopted along with his sister, Hannah. They're twins."

"Sebastian and Theodore are twins too. Fraternal."

"I suspect they'll have a lot in common to build on. Maybe they'll become great friends."

Calliope gave a small smile and nodded her head. "I hope so."

"Calliope, this is Bohannon, Sword, Data, and Zora. Zora has been looking into your background. I hope you understand we needed to confirm your story."

She nodded. "Yeah. I suppose you did."

"I haven't spoken to Chase yet," Zora said, "but I've tracked his movements during that time, and I'm sure he was with your sister before the boys were born."

"We also confirmed how you got custody of the boys," Data said. "You were brave to take that on at such a young age."

"It was the only option," I said softly. "I couldn't let them go into foster care."

"No," Carnage said, "you couldn't. You didn't. I'm sure when Chase gets here he'll appreciate your position and respect you and the boys enough not to upend your lives."

I looked up at Carnage. He wasn't looking at me. He was looking at Cain.

Cain nodded. "I'm sure he'll consider everything. I hope you'd allow him the chance to get to know his sons, should he want to do so?"

I shivered, wrapping my arms around myself,

trying not to burst into tears. I felt like they were trying to bully me into something they weren't sure I'd want to do. And, honestly, I wasn't sure how I felt about any of this. "I -- I won't let him or anyone take my boys away. I won't."

"No one said you had to, Calliope," Carnage growled. Surprisingly, he stepped closer, putting an arm around me. "We'll work out something with Chase, but the boys are yours. Legally."

"You gave up your own childhood for them," Angel said. "Didn't you?"

I met Angel's gaze. I was confused, but Angel seemed to know like no one else did. "I don't know I'd say *that*, but I devoted myself to trying to protect them."

"How'd you end up with the guy you were with when our group found you?"

"Cain." Angel turned to look at her husband. "That's not fair."

"It is. We need to know."

"That's not your business," I said, shrugging off Carnage. "I got us into a dangerous situation I didn't know how to deal with, and I needed help. While I appreciate you being there when I desperately needed it, my custody of the boys is not something you get to decide."

"Why not go to the police?"

"She did," Zora said immediately. "She had a restraining order out on the guy, but that doesn't always work."

"Why did you leave with him?" Cain asked, keeping his gaze focused on me. The look in his eyes made me shrink back a little, even when I tried to stand my ground.

Again, Carnage put an arm around me, pulling

me solidly against his body. "Cain," he said warningly.

"Not another word, Carnage," Cain snarled, never taking his eyes off me. "If I'm keeping a club member away from his kids, I want to know they're safe. And that their guardian has more than two brain cells to rub together."

That got my back up. "Spoken like a man who has no lack of friends," I snapped. "I just wanted some male companionship, OK? A guy who could be a father to the boys. They need a strong male influence in their lives. I thought Mark was a good guy. He was at first, but things changed pretty quick. By the time I realized he was only after any money I had, he already had his claws in deep. He told me he'd hurt the boys unless I did what he wanted. He controlled my finances. Not just the insurance money my sister left me for the boys, but everything I had coming in from the three jobs I worked. I tried to leave more than once. The last time…" I trailed off with a sob. "The last…"

"He threatened them, didn't he?" Zora asked softly.

"He held a knife to Theodore's throat while he slept. Only, that was when Theo really started to change. I'm afraid he was awake the entire time."

"You could have just taken the boys and run," Cain insisted, pushing me when my back was already against the wall.

"I tried once, but the car was in his name, and he reported it stolen! I got dragged back, and he had the boys overnight while I was in jail. If I'd done it again and gotten caught…"

"That's enough," Angel told Cain. "No more."

Cain gave her an annoyed look but backed off. "I needed to know, Angel. You know I did."

"There are other ways of going about it," Angel

snapped, pulling me into her arms, away from Carnage, and hugging me tightly. It was almost enough to break me. Almost. I wanted to cry. God, I wanted to sob until all this pressure inside was gone.

"I found where the auto theft charge was filed against her," Zora said. "She's telling the truth, Cain."

"Why is it always the women defending themselves against the big bad bikers?" Angel sounded very angry. "Did you ever think to question Chase before you beat up an already beaten young woman? If this is all for your precious patched member, maybe I need to rethink how much I want to be associated with the whole lot of you."

"Angel," Cain said warningly. "This is club business."

"Bullshit! This is about a young woman and the children she's raised since they were infants. *When she was just sixteen*!" She pulled away from me and turned to her husband. "You'd think after all this time you'd have learned to behave better than this. If you're not going to defend her, I certainly will. You give me equal time with Chase, and I'll call it good."

"Don't do it, Cain," Data said softly. "She'll tear that boy apart."

"Like he just tore Calliope apart," Angel countered. "And you," she pointed at Data. "You knew she was just trying to survive. If Zora had all that information, you had it too."

"I'm just trying to keep any more innocents from being hurt," Data said, raising his hands in defense.

"You're making it worse, Data." Carnage snagged my hand and tugged me closer. I wasn't sure how to feel about that. It seemed like both Angel and Carnage were solidly on my side, but who could really tell? Angel, yeah. I could see that. But Carnage? Was this all some kind of game to see what I'd tell them? I hated games. I was never any good at them.

Cain scrubbed a hand over his face. "Angel, I didn't mean to make it sound like any of this is Calliope's fault."

"You could have fooled me." Angel leaned her palms on Cain's desk and looked him in the eyes. "This girl needs our help. Not your accusations."

"Well aware of that." He sighed. "I'm sorry, Calliope. I needed answers before I said anything to Chase. I'm not used to questioning women."

"I understand," I said, just wanting to get out of here before I broke down. As it was, I was trembling so hard, there was no way Carnage didn't notice. "May I go? Theodore especially won't like me out of his sight for long."

"Yes. Go to your boys. I'll have Angel and Zora open a suite for the three of you. Would you feel better close to Carnage?"

"Yes." Carnage didn't give me a chance to reply. "Put her in the rooms across from mine. It's got two bedrooms, but they're big enough for two full-sized beds in each one."

"Give the women an hour. Then get them settled. Data, you and Zora are keeping an eye on that Mark guy. Right?"

Zora nodded her head. "Mark Johnson. He's using her credit card. If he makes a move in this direction, we'll know it well in advance." She laid a hand on Calliope's shoulder. "I promise you'll be safe here. These guys are really good people. The whole club is." She gave Cain a glance under her lashes before adding, "Most of the time."

I just nodded, my gaze going to the floor. I'd never felt more defeated in my life. I wanted to lean on

Carnage, to turn to him and cry against his chest, but I didn't know him that well. If he rejected me, I'd look like an even bigger fool. Worse, if he followed his president as blindly as Chase seemed to have back in the day, I risked letting him tear my family apart.

Which brought up another question. Why did I feel such a pull toward the big, tattooed biker? He was just as gruff as the rest of them. Maybe it was because he'd recognized I needed help and got me out of a bad situation. Maybe it was the way he'd taken care of me when I'd puked so violently on the side of the road. Maybe it was the way he chattered on with Sebastian for four freaking hours on the way to the compound and never once complained.

Whatever it was, I wanted to be near him. Other than Angel, I felt like he was the only one here who would give a damn what happened to me and the boys. Whatever it was, I needed to nip it quickly. I'd end up hurting all of us if I didn't.

Chapter Three
Carnage

In the twenty-plus years I'd known Cain, there had never been a time when I'd wanted to kill my friend and boss. If we'd been alone, if I hadn't known both Bohannon and Sword would have killed me rather than let me harm Cain, I would have happily slit the motherfucker's throat. I got what Cain was trying to do, but there were other ways to go about it.

What surprised me most was, first, that Calliope had put up with it, answering his questions as best she could, and second, that Angel had stood up to her husband the way she had. That second almost made me smile. Almost. I'd be sure to ask Cain how he was sleeping at night. Or where. Because I had a feeling there was a couch in his very near future.

Right now, I escorted Calliope firmly by the hand to the backyard where the kids were all playing. From the looks of things, Sebastian had jumped right in, not missing a beat. Even Theodore was participating, if a bit more sedately.

"I'm so sorry to have put you guys out," Calliope said softly. "We can go to a hotel or something. You don't have to put us up here."

"Not another word," I snarled. "That was a bullshit thing Cain did, and he knows it."

"I meant what I said. I won't let Chase or anyone else take the boys away from me. I realize he needs a chance to get to know them, but he's not completely innocent here. He knew they hadn't used protection, so there was a possibility she might be pregnant, and he left without a backward glance. Cherry said she had her lawyer try to get in touch with him after she found out she had cancer." She sighed, sounding defeated.

"The least he could have done was follow up to make sure she wasn't carrying his child."

"How long has it been since you had a good night's sleep?" It was an abrupt change of subject, but I needed to distract her. She looked like she was about to fall down with fatigue.

She looked away. "A while." Then her gaze snapped back to me. "But I'm not leaving the boys to go take a fucking nap."

"We're not gonna take them out from under you, Calliope. Chase won't be back for a couple more days. You've got a fight ahead of you no matter what happens, so why not use this time to rest so you've got your wits about you?" I was trying to be reasonable when what I really wanted to do was lock her in the bedroom and hold her still until she stopped fighting and just passed out.

She looked like she wanted to do exactly that. To rest. To just sleep for as long as she could. Then she shook her head. "Not unless the boys are with me."

I wanted to grind my teeth in frustration. "Fuck." Scrubbing a hand over my face, I led her to a lounge chair by the backyard. The girls were there watching the kids play and chatting when we approached.

"Darcy, this is Calliope. She's Theo and Sebastian's mother."

Darcy stood and welcomed Calliope with a hug. "It's so good to meet you! Does Sebastian ever meet a stranger?"

Thankfully, Calliope smiled. "Not many."

"They both seem like sweet boys. Theodore seems a little reserved, but I think he's enjoying being around Gunnar."

"He's been through a lot recently," Calliope admitted softly. "I hope they're not being a bother."

"Oh, heavens no! Gunner is happy to have them so he's finally got the upper hand on all the girls. Won't you come sit with me for a while?"

"Actually," I interrupted, "I need to collect the boys. They've all had a long day. Thought they might want to rest for a while before dinner."

"That sounds like a good idea." Darcy called the kids over.

Theodore was the first one back, his gaze fixed squarely on his mother. "You OK, Mom?"

"I'm fine, sweetie."

"Your mom needs a nap," I said without preamble. "She'd rest better if the two of you were with her. You think you could play video games or watch TV in the room I've got for you?"

Sebastian shrugged. "Sure. Can Gunnar come with us?"

"I'll ask their parents, but I'm sure it will be fine." I shot off a text to Cain. As angry as I was at the man, I wouldn't bypass him and go to his wife. Not with regard to their children, even with something as simple as this. The reply was fast.

"Cain says it's fine." I held out my hand for Calliope. "I'll take you to your room. You can get settled, and I'll sit with the boys while you rest. You can leave the door open to your bedroom, but you *will* take a nap."

"I couldn't possibly --"

"Mom," Theo said, moving closer to her. "I promise I won't let anyone take us away. You need a nap."

"Eight going on thirty-eight," she muttered. "Fine. But only for an hour."

Theo just nodded and took her hand, giving me the stink eye. Yeah, he knew I was moving in on their mother, and he was having none of it. Which was good. It helped me keep my perspective. I didn't need to fall further under her spell. Or the boys'. I already found myself protective as fuck. I was too close to the situation and wasn't sure I could keep myself at a distance. Because, if Chase proved he had no knowledge of the children, it was possible -- no matter how much I promised Calliope -- Cain would let him push a claim on the boys. If that happened, I knew Calliope would never forgive me. And it was quite possible Theodore would cut my throat in my sleep.

On the way to their room, I stopped by Data's office where he and Zora were busy at their "command center." It consisted of a bank of computer displays with all kinds of shit I had no hope of understanding. Hell, I didn't *want* to understand, really. It got them information. Gave me a headache. End of story.

"Hey. Getting our girl and her boys settled?"

"Not your girl," I growled. "But I need a gaming system. Boys are gonna play with Gunnar while Calliope takes a nap. Can you hook them up in their room?"

"Give me ten minutes," Data said. "I got just the thing."

That done, I ushered everyone to the room across from mine where Angel was just exiting. She smiled warmly, urging the boys inside where they immediately started exploring.

"This should get you started," Angel said. "There're some toiletries in the bathroom, including new toothbrushes and hairbrushes and such. I wasn't sure what everyone had by way of clothing, but I tucked some packages of underwear and socks in the drawers for you and the boys. If you need more pillows or extra blankets, or anything else, really, let me know." She looked at me. "You make sure she has my number."

"I'll take care of it."

"I'm so sorry about Cain," Angel said, looking away. Her brows drew together. I couldn't remember ever seeing her this angry at her husband since they'd met. "He's a good man. Even better president to these guys. But he's extremely protective. I imagine he was trying to think how he'd feel if I'd run off with his kids."

"Cherry didn't run off," Calliope said softly but defensively. "Chase ran away from her. I stand by what I said in there. Even if Cherry lied. If she didn't try to find him. Chase knew they had had unprotected sex. If he'd been interested in any children he might have, he should have checked to make sure she hadn't gotten pregnant."

"Honey," Angel said, snagging her hand and squeezing. "I'm on your side. How much access Chase has -- if any -- should be your decision. You've raised those boys entirely on your own. Chase doesn't get a say unless you give him one."

"I appreciate that." Calliope was folding in on herself. It made me want to punch something. I could tell by the look on Angel's face when she looked up at me she had some very harsh feelings as well.

"Try to get a little rest, Calliope. I'll come get you guys for dinner. I think the boys are grilling out tonight, so it will be burgers and hotdogs. Maybe some chicken, but they say chicken is for pussies, so who knows." She smiled, obviously trying to lighten the mood, but Calliope had reached her limit. I could see tears trying to form in her eyes.

"Thank you. We'd appreciate the meal."

Angel nodded, then looked up at me again. The

look she gave me made me realize exactly why the woman was our president's ol' lady. It was a look Cain often had when he wanted to be obeyed at all costs. "Take care of her."

"All over that, ma'am."

Angel snorted. "Ma'am," she muttered. "I'm not a fucking *ma'am*."

That got a giggle from Calliope and a soft smile from Angel. Then I ushered Calliope inside the suite. I took her straight to the bedroom. The boys could be heard laughing and talking in the other room right before Data came in, followed by a couple of the prospects, some bigass gaming system in tow. Must have been something special because I could hear Sebastian "oohing" and "ahhing" from the other room.

"Sounds like Data has just the thing to keep them occupied for a while." I walked around the room checking out the windows and making sure the bathroom was empty. Force of habit. I always checked out a room before settling in.

"You expecting someone to be hiding out?" Calliope looked curious, but also vulnerable and afraid.

"No, baby." I winced. The "baby" thing had just slipped out. Clearing my throat, I continued. "Habit I picked up in the Marines."

"I suppose it's a good habit to have."

"I suppose." There was an awkward silence. I knew I needed to leave her alone, but I hated leaving her like this. She was so small. The events of the day were obviously catching up to her, and she'd reached her limit of brave today. She needed someone to take over, but I didn't think she'd let me. Probably wouldn't let anyone from the club, including the women. "Do you want me to stay with you? Watch over you?"

She didn't say a word, just shook her head, looking down at the floor. OK. I'd had enough. Calliope needed sleep, and I knew there was no way she'd do it on her own.

"I'll be right back."

I left the room to find Theodore. The boy was sitting on the couch, watching the other two boys with interest, but not making a move to join their gaming. "Theodore," I said softly, jerking my head in an indication for Theo to come to me. Immediately, Theodore got off the couch and crossed the room.

"Mom OK?"

"No." No use sugarcoating it. Besides, as much as I wanted to protect the boys, to make them act like boys instead of men, this wasn't the time. Theo was already too grown up and he had the same need -- probably stronger -- to protect Calliope that I was rapidly developing. "She needs sleep."

"Yeah. She never sleeps unless Mark is gone. Then she only naps."

"She's not gonna sleep unless she knows you guys are safe."

"She's afraid that Chase guy's gonna come and take us away." Theodore shook his head. "I ain't gonna let him."

"Me neither, kid." I scrubbed a hand over my face. "She needs someone with her right now. Someone to actually make her lie down. I know it's a lot to ask, but…"

"I'll lay down with her," Theo said automatically. "It sometimes helps her sleep."

For some fucking reason, my fucking chest swelled with pride. This wasn't my kid. Hell, I'd just met Theodore a few hours ago. But I was so fucking proud of the boy I wanted to beat my chest and declare to the world, "That's my boy!" But he wasn't. And Calliope wasn't my woman.

"Thanks. If you need me, I'll be in here with Sebastian and Gunnar. Don't hesitate to call out if she gets distressed. Don't try to do it all yourself. Only reason I'm askin' is because I know she won't let me, and she shouldn't. She doesn't know me, and I'm in a club with a man she sees as a threat."

Theodore looked me up and down, then nodded. "You might not be as bad as I first thought." Then he walked into the room, leaving the door open. I watched as he went to Calliope, sat on the bed beside her and put an arm around her. Soon he'd coaxed her to lie down with him. She pulled the boy into her arms, and they settled down. While I stood there, watching her drift off, Theo looked at me and nodded once before sighing and shutting his eyes. The sight broke my heart the same as it warmed it. These boys loved Calliope same as she loved them. I decided right then and there, if Chase Dutton wanted to fight for custody of these kids, I'd kill the fuckin' prick before I'd let him draw another breath.

* * *

Calliope

I woke up confused and disoriented. It was full dark. Silvery moonlight streamed in through a window on the far side of the room. Turning my head, I saw a door cracked open with a muted golden light spilling from it. Bathroom? The second that thought hit my mind I needed to pee. I was also stiff. Probably because I woke up in the same position I fell asleep in…

Except Theodore wasn't with me.

I sat bolt upright. "Theo!" I yelled for my son as I tried to scramble from the bed. A big hand gripped my shoulder and tried to push me back onto the bed.

"Easy, girl. Easy."

"Where's my son!"

"Asleep in his own room with his brother. I'll take you to check on him if you like." That was Carnage. His voice was sleep roughened. Husky. For some reason that hit me hard with a sexy punch. He could easily have been waking up beside me. He let me up, backing off but not leaving me completely.

In the dark, I heard the chair rustle against his clothes as he stood. His silhouette was big and imposing. The whole scene struck me as surreal. It was like I was in a dream world where monsters were near and had my family. "It's OK," he said again. "I'll take you to them. Here. Take my hand."

I could just barely make out where he held his hand out to me. Hesitantly, I took it, not really wanting to touch him, but needing to see my boys. The second I touched him I knew I was in trouble. It wasn't a bad thing. Quite the opposite. His rough hand closed over mine gently. Warmly. He felt familiar. Like a safe place in the cold dark, ironic as it sounded.

When I stood, he let go of my hand only to put his arm around my shoulders. The heat radiating from him was comforting when I didn't want it to be. He was potentially the enemy. If Chase decided to challenge me for custody of the boys, I had no doubt Carnage would deliver carnage to our lives. The fallout might kill me. Because I knew Theodore would fight, no matter how badly the odds were stacked against him. The boy was as fierce as they came, and he could get physically hurt. Would this man be the one to hurt him?

Try as I might, I couldn't convince myself of all that. I knew better than to put much stock in his promises, but Carnage wasn't a bad man. It was only by an unhappy coincidence I'd landed with him in the first place. If Chase had belonged to any club other than this one, I had no doubt everything Carnage promised about keeping us together and safe would be real. But Chase was a member. So I had no expectation his club could or would stop him from trying to take my boys.

Carnage helped me out of one bedroom and to the other side of the suite to the room where the boys were sleeping. Sebastian was sitting up in the bed, the blanket covering his bent knees as he played a handheld video game. Theodore was on his side, but raised up when he heard us approach.

"Mom?" Theo's voice alerted Sebastian they weren't alone, and he looked up from his game. "Everything OK?"

"Yeah," I said, sagging against Carnage in relief. "I just woke up confused…"

"I'm sorry," Theodore shoved the covers back and sat up on the bed. "I didn't want to bother you after supper, so I didn't come back to bed."

"No!" I said, putting my hands out in front of me, a gesture for him to stay in bed. "Don't get up. It's fine. I just… I forgot where I was."

"You thought someone took us," Theo said in an all-too-understanding voice. "Don't worry, Mom. I know you think I'm too young to fight, but I promise I won't let anyone take me or Sebastian."

"Besides," Sebastian piped up. "Cain said we didn't have to go anywhere we didn't want to. And we wanna stay with you."

Theo stood, despite my urging him not to, and crossed to me, putting his arms around me. He hugged me for a long time, then pulled back. "I know better than to believe everything adults say. I'm still on guard. No matter how nice they are to us." He looked up at me, then gave Carnage a glance. The boy wasn't apologetic about it either. He meant for Carnage to understand the big man's words meant little to him.

"You're a brave, intelligent young man, Theo. You'll make a good MC president one day."

Theo didn't acknowledge Carnage. Just looked back up at me. "Do you want me to stay with you awhile, Mom? I can come back to bed after you get to sleep."

"No, Theo. I'm not that helpless." I knew I was blushing bright red. Thank God for the dark. "I'm fine on my own."

"I know," Theo said. "But you worry about us. You know, we can camp out in your room. It wouldn't take much to make a bed on the floor."

"I'm fine. Really."

"I'll get a couple of inflatable beds," Carnage said. "We can set them up in your room and you boys can camp out."

"Can we make a blanket fort?" Sebastian asked, the light from his game highlighting the excited look on his face.

I felt Carnage shrug. "Don't see why not. Give me a minute to get some supplies. Theo, can you heat up your mother's supper?"

"Sure." Then everyone was getting out of bed.

"Wait! You don't have to do this. I'm fine. And I'm not hungry. What time is it?"

"Not even midnight," Carnage said. "You need to eat, and I don't think either of the boys were asleep. If this puts your mind at ease, it's worth a little effort on our part to take care of you."

Theo nodded. "He's right. Besides, I think it'd be

fun to make a fort. It'd be like being in a separate room, but we're still with you."

"I feel like an idiot," I muttered, turning to go back to my room and change my shirt. I'd slept in it and my shorts. While I wasn't concerned about the shorts, I was sure my T-shirt smelled funny. Until right then, I hadn't paid attention. Now? With Carnage standing beside me, his arm still around my shoulders, I was acutely aware. He was definitely close enough to smell my sleep sweat.

I turned to shut the door while I changed, but Carnage was hot on my heels. I could hear the boys in the kitchen area, talking as they worked. I backed up a couple of steps, and he entered the room, closing the door behind me.

"Now. Talk. Why do you feel like an idiot?" That was the last question I expected him to ask.

"My kids are up at midnight. Fixing me supper. Getting ready to make a blanket fort in my room so I don't have a panic attack when I wake and they're not with me. My *eight-year-old* kids. Theodore acts more like a protector than a child. I've made such a mess of their lives I wouldn't blame Chase for taking them away from me."

Carnage's hand shot out, gripping my chin and tilting my head up. He didn't hurt me, but I could feel the anger in his touch. "You listen to me, Calliope." He bared his teeth at me slightly. His voice was soft, but he wasn't pleased at all. "This isn't your fault. So you chose an asshole boyfriend. You can't know someone for sure until you spend time with them. Sounds like he pushed his way into your life, then things went horribly wrong. You're not responsible for the actions of others."

"Your president said it himself. I should have left

sooner than I did. They're gonna let Chase do whatever he wants, and I can't say I really blame them!"

"Stop!" he snarled. "Just stop it!" He slid his hand to the back of my head, his other hand still gripping my chin and forcing me to look up at him. "I will not let anyone take those boys away from you. I talked with the two of them at supper. Cain was there, too. You just saw the boys. Did they act like they were scared of me?"

I shook my head. "No."

"We weren't mean. We didn't pressure them or push them or in any way make them feel like we wanted to take them away from you. You can ask them once we get them settled and I'm in the other room. Get me?"

"O-OK. What… what are you getting at?"

"Those boys belong with you. I agree with you Chase had his chance. Even if your sister lied and he knew nothing of her pregnancy or her cancer. He knew he hadn't used protection. So fuck it all. I'm on your side and always will be."

We looked at each other for long moments. His eyes seemed to flicker in his anger, a golden-amber flame. The dominant way he held me, the strength in his grip should have scared me, or at the very least made me uneasy. Instead, I found myself strangely aroused. I think it was the intensity of his gaze. It was like he was willing me to believe him and believe him with a passion I'd never falter with. When I moistened my lower lip, he swore.

"Fuck," he whispered, his grip tightening. "Do that again."

"Do what?" My skin erupted in sweat. My breathing came faster, and my gaze fastened on his lips.

"Wet those lovely lips. Ready yourself for my kiss."

"Oh, God…" But I did exactly what he asked, darting my tongue out to wet my lips. With a groan, Carnage descended on me, his lips covering mine in a sensual but dominant kiss.

I was reminded of an old movie I dearly loved. *There are kisses, then there are kisses. This one fell into the latter category.* When Carnage swept his tongue into my mouth, my whole world narrowed to nothing but him. We could have been in a room full of people, and I wouldn't have cared as long as he kept kissing me. His masculine scent surrounded me, embedded in my senses and filled me with… him. Carnage. I already knew he was a force of nature, but nothing could have prepared me for this.

That moan of need couldn't have come from me. Could it? It must have, because Carnage growled, letting go of my head to wrap an arm around me and pull me close to him. He still gripped my chin, but somehow it felt right. I liked the domination. Craved it, even. I was a firework out of control, exploding in the night.

All too soon, Carnage ended the kiss, his hand still holding my chin, keeping me right where he wanted me. He looked down at me, a look of satisfaction and lust blazing in those heavy-lidded eyes.

"Calliope…" He murmured my name. Whispered it like a prayer in its reverence. "Sweet as honey."

"Why did you do that?" I hadn't meant to voice the question, but I needed an answer.

"Been wanting to do it since I first saw you.

You're still too fragile for much, but I'll get to all that fire inside you soon. Once you get comfortable here, you'll feel stronger."

The statement had the effect of a bucket of ice water. "Just because I made some bad decisions in my life doesn't mean I'm weak."

"Not at all. But you're feeling the pain of some of those decisions. Been there myself, so I get you. You're exhausted and, no matter how tough you are, you've been beaten down by someone bigger than you. You're scared and off-balance, but we'll soon take care of that. I'm telling you right now, when you're feeling more like yourself, I'm gonna take you to bed and not let you up until you're screamin' my name at the top of your lungs."

My knees gave out. Had Carnage not had such a hold on me, I'd have fallen. Clinging to his shoulders, I tried to get a hold of myself. Mark had been the first man I'd ever been with, and only a few times. This man was out of my league in every possible way. "I mistook loneliness for affection once, Carnage. I'm not doing it again."

"I get that. And I'm not pushing you. Yet. But once you figure out the situation here with you, the boys, and Chase, you're gonna think about that kiss, and you're gonna want more. When you do, come to me. I'll be ready and waiting for you."

Slowly, with exquisite gentleness, Carnage let me go. He made sure I could stand on my own, then gave me a cocky grin before he left me to change. When he shut the door, it was all I could do to not crumple to the floor. He was wrong about one thing. I wasn't sure I wanted to wait to see what happened with everything here. I wanted him to finish what that kiss promised.

I went to the bathroom, relieved myself, then

washed my hands, splashing cold water on my face when I was done. I was so fucked. I only thought I knew about sex. I realized now I'd only scratched the surface with Mark. Hell, I'd barely gotten rid of my virginity if that kiss from Carnage was any indication.

I changed shirts and headed to the kitchen. It was the last place I wanted to be, though I knew I had to. The boys would be disappointed if I didn't eat. I'd learned that they liked doing things for me. Theodore had started doing chores around the house, which had prompted Sebastian to do the same. They always preened under the praise I heaped on them when everything was done when I came home. Lord knew Mark never did anything.

Sure enough, when I got to the kitchen, the boys stood there expectantly, waiting for my approval on the meal. Though I really didn't want to eat, it looked good, and there was no way I'd disappoint them.

"Oh, my," I said with a grin. "This looks and smells delicious."

"We just heated it up," Sebastian said. "But we made the plate for you in case you woke up hungry."

"You have no idea how much I appreciate that," I said, reaching for them. Both boys came into my arms, hugging me. "Thank you so much, guys."

I ate while Sebastian talked. Carnage encouraged the talk and tried to get Theodore to say more. Surprisingly, the child told me about their afternoon, playing games with Gunnar.

"I think I like it here, Mom," Theo said softly. "Not because of the games and stuff, but I like the people." He glanced at Sebastian. "It feels safe."

"Yeah," Sebastian added with a scowl. "Not like when that asshole Mark came home. These guys would pound him if he hit you."

I ducked my head. "I'm so sorry, guys. I messed up bringing Mark into our lives."

Sebastian shrugged. "He was OK at first. I liked him."

"Me too," Theodore agreed. They had liked him. For a couple of weeks. Then the trouble had started.

"What's this Chase guy like, Mom? Is he an asshole like Mark?"

I shook my head. "Not at all. In fact, you'll probably like him." It took a lot to admit that. It was the truth, but I had some hard feelings.

"If he's such a good guy," Theodore asked, his gaze leveled on me. "Then why did he leave us?"

With a sigh, I shook my head. "Me and your birth mom weren't exactly nice to him. He probably thought he didn't have a choice. That we wouldn't want him in your lives." Theodore just shook his head, as if he wasn't buying it.

"All right," Carnage interrupted. "I think it's time for bed. While your mom's finishing up, let's go make your fort."

"Are you staying with us tonight?" Sebastian looked at Carnage, a hopeful expression on his face.

"I might stay in the living room. You can leave the door open if you want. But I'll give you and your mom some privacy."

"You can stay in Mommy's room with us if you want." Sebastian looked from Carnage to Theodore. Probably hoping to get some support from Theo.

"Yeah," his brother agreed, surprising me. "You could stay with Mom. Make sure she's OK."

Carnage shook his head. "Afraid that's your job tonight. If she needs someone, you'll be right there."

Theodore pursed his lips disapprovingly. "If you say so." Then he turned to go into the bedroom.

"Finish up," Carnage said as he laid a hand on my shoulder. Then he leaned in and kissed my temple. I shivered in awareness, unable to compartmentalize that kiss we'd shared. I wanted to see what would happen if I let this guy have me. I mean, it wasn't happening. That was obvious. But I wanted it to. Carnage, on the other hand, seemed confident he'd get me to yes. The only question was when.

Once the boys were gone, I cleaned up my supper. Hadn't been very hungry anyway. Too much to think about. My life was on a roller coaster, and I had no idea how to get off. I took my time going back to my room. I needed the boys close, but I needed some time on my own to think.

When I wandered into the bedroom, I found Carnage and the boys putting the finishing touches on the blanket fort. Sebastian was tucking a sleeping bag and pillow on one side while Theo crawled into his on the other.

"Are you sure you won't stay with us?" Sebastian was using his best wheedling voice on Carnage. I'd heard that voice many times over the years.

"Sorry, kid. Your mama wouldn't want me in here."

"Why not? Mark stayed with her all the time. And you're way better'n him."

"That's different, Sebastian. Right now, it needs to be you guys and your mom. I'll be in the other room, though. All you have to do is call out or come get me."

"Whatever," Theo said, covering up and lying down, his back to Carnage.

"Theodore," I chastised gently. "It's better if he sleeps in the other room."

"No, it's not. When he's here, we're all safe. He's

not like Mark. He's not a taker. He's a protector. If you keep him out, he can't protect us."

Carnage knelt down by the opening of their tent. "You listen to me, kid. I'll always protect you. I don't have to be in the same room with you to do that. Especially when you're here. This whole club will keep you safe, Theo." He said it with such conviction, even I believed it. My heart wanted to sing, but I knew better than to read more into it than it was. Deep down, Carnage was a white knight. We were in distress, and he was charging to our rescue. I'd even had that same thought before. Carnage was our white knight. Once we were safe, Carnage's interest would fade. We'd be safe but alone. He'd move on.

"It's fine, Theo. He'll just be in the other room."

"If we need him, we can go get him?" Sebastian looked from me to Carnage.

"Absolutely. You need me quick, you just holler out. I'll hear you."

Sebastian nodded. "All right." Theodore didn't acknowledge either of us.

Carnage turned to go. "Leave the door open."

I nodded, but followed him to the door. I had no idea why I did, but I couldn't seem to stop myself. I wanted him to stay. With me. In my bed. I just wanted him near. Where I could touch him when I needed to.

"I'll be right here, Calliope." Carnage reached out and cupped my cheek, stroking his thumb across my lower lip. Then he leaned in and gently brushed his lips over mine before turning to leave.

Chapter Four
Carnage

Leaving Calliope in that room with her boys had been hard. I wanted to stay with them, to be there if any of them had nightmares or just woke up scared in a strange place. I reasoned with myself that the boys had each other and I'd never be able to stay out of Calliope's bed if I stayed. I wasn't sure why Theo was angry with me, but I suspected he just wanted his mother not to be alone.

As I lay on the couch, one arm behind my head and looking out the sliding patio door at the moon shining through the glass, I thought about how much I wanted to be in there with Calliope. She had to be terrified. I could see she was trying very hard to believe me when I told her I'd never let anyone take her kids away, but I could also see flashes of hurt because she thought I would always side with my club. The fact was… yeah. Until I met Calliope, I'd have done whatever Cain told me to without question. But if my president told me to convince Calliope to let Chase have access to those boys now, I knew there was no way I'd do it.

Calliope was a surprise. Sure, I'd met her under less-than-ideal circumstances, but she was a remarkable woman. The more I was around her, the more I wanted her. That kiss tonight was the beginning of the end for me. I'd probably kissed hundreds of women in my time. None of them compared to the innocent enthusiasm Calliope showed me. She wasn't looking for what I could give her -- materially or physically. She was simply riding the sensations I shoved at her. Never would she have kissed me on her own, but she welcomed my kisses when I gave them to her. She was clever, strong, and protective of those kids, and that put her high in my estimation.

When Cain and Angel had dinner with me and the boys, it was to get a feel for what their life was like. Cain had walked his way skillfully through the boys where he'd botched his interview with Calliope. I was pretty sure Angel was the reason for his gentleness with the boys. Though Cain and Angel were both parents, Cain could still be abrasive at times. His kids would roll their eyes and call him "cranky Daddy." Theodore and Sebastian wouldn't have reacted in the same way. They'd have equated his actions with what they were familiar with. Their mother's boyfriend, Mark.

All this ran around in my head, making sleep impossible. I'd just sat up, thinking about going outside and sitting on the patio and listening to the breeze rustling through the leaves when Theo walked into the room. He was so quiet he almost got the drop on me. Hell, if I'd been dozing, he would have been on me before I was aware he was anywhere around.

"Carnage?"

"What's wrong, Theo?" My instinct was to stand, to ready myself, but I didn't want to intimidate the kid.

"You need to go stay with Mom." Little did the kid know that was exactly where I wanted to be.

"She OK?"

"No. She's crying." Theo looked back over his shoulder in the direction of his mother, as if he could see her even now. "She's trying to be quiet so we won't hear, and Sebastian's asleep. But I hear her."

"Why don't you crawl into bed with her? Like you did this afternoon."

He shook his head. "When I do she tries to comfort me instead of the other way around because

I'm just a kid." He shrugged as if it wasn't a big deal, but I could tell he didn't like it that she wouldn't let him help her because he was young. I wanted to tell him it wasn't because he was young but because she was his mom. It was her instinct to protect him from everything, but that wouldn't help my case here. The very last place I needed to be was in Calliope's bed. Not now.

I scrubbed a hand through my hair and over my face. "She probably doesn't want me there, Theo. A man doesn't climb into a woman's bed without her permission."

"When my mom cries, you should do everything you can to make her *not* cry. No matter what she wants. Besides, unless you plan on hurtin' her, she gets what's best for her. Not what she wants." Now, that was an ultimatum if ever I heard one. And I like the kid's way of thinking. Protect my woman at all costs? I could do that.

"What are you sayin', kid?" It was time to get down to business. For some reason, Theo had decided he wanted me in their lives, though it was impossible to tell for how long he intended for me to be there or why. I needed to find out both, so I could decide how to move forward.

"You need to be with our mom. To take care of her and Sebastian."

"What about you?"

He waved me off. "I can take care of myself. I can take care of my mom, too, but she don't think so. So I need you to be there until I'm older."

That nearly made me laugh. "You know, you can't just haul me into your lives, then dump me when you think you're old enough to be your mom's protector. I get involved with your lives now, I intend on stayin' there a while. And you won't have a say in when I go. Only me and Calliope."

Theo nodded. "That might be OK. If you make it so she ain't sad and crying. I don't like it when Mom cries."

"I take it Mark made her cry."

He nodded. "All the time. I hate him."

"Understandable." I sighed. "All right, kid. You go back to bed. I'll try to comfort your mom. But just remember. You asked for this."

"Make her smile. I like it when she smiles. It's like the whole world lights up."

The kid was killing me.

I gave him a minute to get settled, then crept into the room. Sure enough, I could see Calliope's small form shivering under the covers. She must have been lost in her own thoughts, because she gave a soft gasp and started when I sat on the bed next to her. The silvery moonlight filtering through the window hit her face, and I felt like I'd been hit in the bollocks.

The girl was ethereally lovely. All but the tears leaking from her eyes. Her eyes sparkled with moisture and her plump lips were parted. It looked like her teeth had abraded the bottom one as she tried to keep her weeping silent, because it was puffy and red.

"What's wrong?" Her whispered question made my chest ache. If ever there was a girl who needed saving it was this one. She was on edge. Wound up. She needed to relax. In order for that to happen, she needed to feel safe. As long as the question of Chase and his claim on the kids remained out there, she'd never have that. Especially not in the Bones clubhouse.

"Was gonna ask you the same thing." I brushed a lock of hair off her forehead. "You're crying."

"I'm so sorry," she said, and several big

teardrops spilled from her eyes again. "I didn't mean to wake you up."

"You didn't. Thought I'd check on you. Glad I did." Not a lie, but I didn't want to out Theo either. "Scooch over."

"What?" She looked adorably confused. I didn't give her much of a choice as I climbed into bed with her. I stayed on top of the covers but pulled her into my arms just the same. "Carnage," she gasped, glancing at the tent where the boys were.

"Don't worry. I'm not gonna embarrass either of us. Just figured you could use some comfort. Don't women like to cuddle and shit when they're upset?"

"Maybe? I don't know. Carnage, you can't --"

"Can. Am."

I got her situated so her back was to my front, her head lying on my arm, my arm around her middle. She was so still for a very long time. Still and stiff.

"This isn't a good idea."

"Because of the boys?"

"Well, yeah. They don't need to see us together like this."

"I'll be gone before they wake. But you need comfort, and I'm not leaving you to cry yourself to sleep in the dark."

Then she did something totally unexpected. Calliope rolled over and buried her face in my shoulder, clutching my shirt while she quietly sobbed. I had no clue what to do. My earlier encounter with her was all about sex and pleasure. This was raw emotion. Her expressing her fear and worry and raw grief to someone she trusted, and I had no idea what to do with the knowledge or the physicality of it. I closed my arms around her, holding her tightly while murmuring to her that everything would be good. I'd make it good, no matter what it took. Thing was, I got the feeling she didn't believe me. Not really. But she wanted to.

"I've got you, sweet Calliope. I'll keep you and the boys safe."

She didn't say anything, just cried until she was spent. Then she lay still in my arms, still clutching my shirt, and slept like the dead. The feeling of this woman in my arms, clinging to me, was a lot to process. It made me feel like I was more than I really was. Made me want to be whatever she needed to take away her pain. This was so out of character for me I wasn't sure what to do. I didn't want to be here like this when Sebastian woke. Hell, I was even squeamish to be here with Theo in the room, but I was hesitant to leave her. Calliope was... special. Just thinking about her younger self taking on the responsibilities of a mother to twins nearly made me ill even as it made my chest swell with pride.

"Mine," I muttered to myself. This woman was mine. At least, she was going to be. It was like flicking some kind of switch in my brain. Where I'd flirted with the idea before, now, there was no denying it.

I lay there, just drifting. I didn't want to go to sleep. Not with the boys still there and their mother in such an intimate position. Didn't mean I wanted to leave her. When I heard the boys stirring in their blanket fort, I raised up slightly. Calliope moaned and tightened her hold on my shirt.

Theo popped his head out of the tent, and his gaze went unerringly to the bed. When he saw me there with Calliope, he gave me a curt nod before urging his brother out of the bedroom. Sebastian glanced back at us and gave me a thumbs-up and a big smile.

"You know where the common room is," I told Theo softly. "Anyone there will help you get breakfast."

"Can we go swimming today?" Sebastian looked hopefully at me.

"Don't see why not. Go get breakfast, and we'll see if we can find you some swimming trunks." Sebastian let out a whoop before clapping his hand over his mouth and glancing at his mother. Then he sprinted for the door. Theo was right behind him. The boy looked at me, then turned the lock on the door before shutting it behind him.

That wasn't creepy or anything. It didn't take much to get what the boy was angling for. He wanted me with his mama so I could protect them all. And I had absolutely no problem with giving this to him. Especially when I wanted Calliope for myself.

"W'asgoin' on?" Calliope pushed up slightly, looking around with wild eyes.

"Shh," I said, petting her back and urging her to lie back down. "The boys'er just goin' for breakfast. You rest here with me a little while longer. 'K?"

She gave a contented groan and stretched, settling her body against mine. For the briefest of moments, I felt like she'd been with me forever. We were a couple waking up on a Saturday morning to our kids hurrying to the living room to watch cartoons or outside to play with friends or some shit. It was so… normal! I'd love to have a kind of normal with her that included pulling her into a dark world of kinky, dirty sex when we were alone. A world where she craved my attention and begged me to make her come over and over. I could easily see her spread out on the bed, hands and feet tied to the corners while I took her any way I wanted to. Just the thought made me harder than a motherfucker. Then she stiffened, and I groaned.

"Fuck," I bit out. "Don't move, Calliope."

"I -- What?"

"You were gonna bolt. Don't you fuckin' move." I tried to use a stern voice, the voice that sent prospects all over the compound scurrying off to do my bidding.

"Why are you still in the bed with me?" Her voice was a high-pitched squeak. It was obvious she was uncomfortable with the situation. "Where are the boys?"

I sighed. "Can't we just go back to the way it was thirty seconds ago? You weren't all flustered then."

"Carnage --"

"Levi," I said.

"What?"

"My name," I said. "Levi Gordon."

She looked up at me, confusion on her lovely face. "Levi?"

I grinned. "Now you're getting it. What's your question?"

She blinked. "Question?"

"That's what I thought. Now. Do you need to go back to sleep for a while or are you ready to start this?"

"Start what?"

Slowly, so I didn't startle her, I rolled us so that I lay half on top of her. I had one thigh between her legs and my upper body covering hers. She sucked in a breath, her lips parting on that little gasp, and her hands flew to my shoulders.

"We're gonna see how we mesh as a couple," I said, giving her a cocky grin I didn't feel. Hell, I felt anything *but* cocky. I was actually nervous as I leaned in to nuzzle her neck. How long had it been since I was nervous about taking a woman? I wasn't even sure I was nervous my very first time. Not like this. And I knew in my heart it was because this woman mattered in whatever way. Not only did I want to make her mine, but she *mattered*.

"What do you mean?" She shivered in my arms as I kissed and nipped her skin, running my lips over her jaw until I found her mouth with mine. I pressed gentle kisses there. Three. Then four.

"You need a man in your life. So do the boys. Consider yourself taken, because I'm claimin' you as my own."

"Don't I get a say?" That was the real sell in this, wasn't it? Did she get a say in this?

"Sure," I said, pulling her more firmly beneath me and moving so that I lay between her thighs. I rocked my hips back and forth, letting her feel my erection. "Tell me you don't want me right now, and I'll leave." I dipped my head back to her neck, letting my beard abrade her delicate skin as I blazed a trail down her neck to the swell of her breast beneath her shirt.

"Carnage!" Her fingers went to my hair where they tunneled and bunched into fists.

"Levi," I reminded gently. "Say it." I pulled away to look her in the eyes. I was inches from her lips, from kissing her again like I had the previous night.

"Levi…"

"Fuck." I took her lips. Instead of the gentle seduction I'd intended, I found myself ravishing her mouth. When she gasped, I swept my tongue inside, taking a long, slow lick, drawing her tongue inside my mouth with kiss after scorching kiss.

I was lost. This wasn't the best time. But, God! I needed Calliope like I needed air. I groaned when she tentatively licked my tongue with her own. Then she sighed contentedly and just surrendered to the overwhelming sensations right along with her.

She slipped her hands over my back and shoulders, bunching my shirt in her fists. I expected some resistance, but she tugged at my shirt until she bunched it up enough to reach bare skin. When she put her palm against my bare back, she sighed into my kiss like the feel of my skin on hers grounded her. Well. I could fix that.

I pulled away to sit back on my heels as she reached for me.

"Relax, baby," I said. "Just losing some clothing. I suggest you do the same."

Her eyes widened. When I pulled off my shirt she reached for me, her hands running over my chest. Tattoos decorated my skin, and I knew that with my ink and muscles, I was a sight to behold.

"Oh, my," she whispered.

"Like what you see?"

"What's not to like? You're beautiful, Levi."

I grinned. "Show me what I'm getting, Calliope. Take off your shirt." It didn't really matter to me what she looked like. I just wanted to get her moving. Because this was happening unless she expressly told me no.

Instead of telling me no or demurring, she nodded her head frantically and squirmed out of her shirt. I chuckled as I lowered myself back to her body, rubbing my chest over her breasts. She arched into my touch, her hands still rubbing across my shoulders and back.

"This feels so good," she whispered. "Never felt so wonderful."

"I ain't even started yet, baby." Finding her mouth again with mine, I kissed her. I needed more and more of her sweet taste, but I needed some answers first. "How many lovers you had?"

"What?"

"You heard me. I need to know how experienced you are before we go further. Don't wanna hurt or frighten you."

She sighed, looking away, almost ashamed. "One," she said softly. "Mark was the only man I'd ever been with"

"Because of your responsibilities?"

She nodded. "I didn't have a great support system. And it never felt right to leave the boys with a sitter for something like going on a date."

"So you waited until they were older." I didn't want her to think I looked down on her for being responsible. Hell, this was the best-case scenario. She had some experience, but not so much I couldn't stake my claim good and proper.

"Yes. I only went out with Mark because I felt like a freak."

I jerked back. That shocked me. "A freak? What the fuck, Calliope?"

"I was twenty-four and a virgin. I felt like I was aging away and drying up inside with no way to unlock all those secrets women have. I mean, sex was this big mystery, and I had no way to explore it."

"What about with me?" I wanted her to talk to me about her feelings. This first time would absolutely be the best fucking time of her life.

Her face turned red, and her breathing shallowed. "After that kiss…" She trailed off, a fine tremor moving through her body as she broke out in a sweat. Voice husky, she continued, "I have a feeling you're about to rock my world."

"That's what I wanted to hear," I said before

taking her lips again.

She moaned into my kiss, opening to accept the thrust of my tongue. I rocked my hips against her, letting her feel how hard I was for her.

"Feel that?"

"Your cock against me?"

I grinned. "That's right, baby. That's my cock. And it's hard for you. You want it inside you?"

She bit her bottom lip, her cheeks tinging pink. "I do, but I'm not sure how responsible --"

"Honey, this is as responsible as it gets. I'll be a good protector for you and the boys. You same as picked me when you picked our club to throw your lot in with. I was the road captain. I made the decision to see what was going on. You came with me. End of story."

"What about Chase? Aren't you afraid I'll use you to keep him away from my kids?"

I shrugged. "Maybe. Still keepin' you. And the boys. Theo trusts me, and I get the feeling he doesn't trust anyone much."

"He didn't used to be that way," she muttered. "He's a good boy."

"Believe me, I'm aware of that. Why do you think I'm in here now? He came and got me last night when you were crying. I'm not stupid enough to think he'd have chosen me if not for the threat of his biological father trying to take him and Sebastian away, but I think he believes that if he can get on my good side, if he can make me love you, I'll keep the three of you together."

"Is he wrong?"

"Only in thinking I have to be with the three of you to make that happen. I don't. And I might try to talk you into letting Chase be in their lives, but I'll never suggest or allow him to just take over. No matter what." I grinned at her. "Now that my agenda is out of the way and you know that I'll help you no matter what, do you still want my cock?"

She nodded her head emphatically. "Yes. Yes, I do."

I chuckled. "Good."

I sat up again, this time tugging at the waistband of her sleep shorts. Tugging the shorts and her panties down her shapely legs, I greedily took in the sight of what I'd soon be claiming.

"Fuck," I growled. "Fuckin' beautiful."

Never taking my eyes from her, I pushed off the bed to drop my lounge pants. My dick bobbed free, slapping my stomach. Calliope's lips parted, and her eyes locked on my cock. She sat up slowly and leaned toward me.

"This probably isn't the best idea I've ever had," she admitted as she reached for my cock. "But I'm not changing my mind."

The second her palm closed around my cock, my body tensed. I grunted, jerking at the exquisite sensation. I'd had dozens of women touch me, give me hand jobs, suck my dick. I'd fucked more women than I could remember. None of them gave me this kind of reaction. None of them made me want to keep them for my own. No one had. Until Calliope.

Instead of slowly jerking me off, Calliope reached for me, kneeling on the bed but bracing her hands on my hips before engulfing my cock head in her mouth.

I cried out, letting my head fall back on my shoulders. My hand went to her head, my fingers bunching in her silky hair. "Fuck… Motherfuck!"

She hummed around me, taking me deep, and

my brain matter scattered. All I could process was the pleasure. The most exquisite sensations imaginable swamped me. She looked up at me, her golden eyes fixed on mine while she swallowed me down. That carnal look was nearly my undoing.

With a growl, I pulled her away from me by her hair, shoving her back onto the bed. She gasped, but the lust filling her eyes told me I hadn't harmed her. Lying back on the bed, she held my gaze, daring me to continue. Afraid I wouldn't?

I bared my teeth at her, pulling her legs apart and pressing them down. "I'm gonna eat you alive, little girl." As my gaze roamed over her bare body, her glistening pussy called to me. "Mine." I must have growled the word, because Calliope tried to close her legs, but I held her firm. "You're mine now, Calliope. I'm takin' you here and keepin' you and your boys with me. You got objections? Give 'em to me now."

She blinked several times and swallowed. Then she lifted her chin defiantly. "We'll stay with you. As long as you're good to us." She pulled her knees up, further baring her pussy to my gaze. "But I'm telling you now. The second my boys see you as a threat, the moment you turn on me or them like Mark did, I'll kill you. Club be damned."

"Just when I thought my dick couldn't get any harder." I winked at her, then lowered my face to her pussy and *feasted*.

* * *

Calliope

I had no idea if Levi's agenda was really what he told me or why he intended to stay in the lives of me and my boys, but I'd take him at face value until he proved not worthy of my trust. He'd been nothing but good to me since I'd first met him. Besides, once his tongue took its first swipe through my pussy, I lost my ever-loving mind. Pleasure was a living thing inside me, my pussy on fire with his intimate kisses. Moisture wept from me, inviting him to take anything he wanted.

"So fuckin' sweet," he growled. "So fuckin' good!"

"Levi! Oh, God!"

My hands flew to his hair, tunneling in and gripping him tightly. I didn't know if I intended to push him away or pull him up my body so he could cover me with all those hard muscles and press me into the bed again. All I knew was I needed more of what he was offering.

Then an orgasm crashed through me, and all I could do was feel. My clit was on fire, my belly contracting with the intense pleasure. I screamed before clapping a hand over my mouth, my ingrained modesty kicking in. If the boys were in the other room, I didn't want them to hear.

"That's it, Calliope. Let go." His voice was as big a temptation as his sinful, tattooed body. Everything about the man screamed sex and carnality. Anything he wanted to give me, I was willing to take as long as I felt this way. Sex had never been like this. Never this all-consuming or necessary. I felt like if he didn't fuck me now, my very life would end in an unfulfilled tangled mass of lust and need.

"Please, please, Levi!"

"You need my cock, baby?"

"Yes! Oh, God! Yes!"

"Then take it." He reached for the nightstand. As far as I knew this room had been empty before I occupied it. But there were condoms in the drawer. He tossed one to me as he raised up once again, sitting back and giving me his cocky smirk. Did I imagine it, or was there strain around his eyes and mouth?

I glanced down at the condom that had landed on my chest. Snagging it, I tore it open and reached for him. Carefully, I fit it over his cock with shaking fingers, rolling it down his impressive length. Once I'd prepared him, Levi lay back on top of me, threading his fingers through mine to hold my hands over my head. Then he kissed me over and over, building my anticipation to a fever pitch.

When the tip penetrated me, I arched, digging my heels into his ass and lifting myself up for more. I cried out, the burn as much an aphrodisiac as anything else.

"Fuck! Stay the fuck still! Goddamn it!" Levi swore viciously at me, but his cock throbbed and pulsed inside me. "I ain't comin' before I'm ready, Calliope! Not on your fuckin' life!"

"I'm coming, Levi!" I screamed as he slid fully inside me. My clit spasmed, triggering my orgasm with an intensity I'd never dreamed of. My whole body tensed, my arms hugging him to me as if I was afraid he was leaving me. I never wanted him to leave me! Never! He alone commanded my body. My experience had to be vastly limited compared to his, but I knew I'd never again feel this level of intensity unless it was him giving it to me.

With a roar to the ceiling, Levi came. His dick pulsed and shuddered, his body glistening with sweat, making his movements over me as he emptied himself inside me slippery with his damp skin. Levi -- Carnage -- wrapped his arms around me and thrust over and over until his movements slowed as he rode out both our orgasms.

Both of us panted, trying to catch our breath. The whole experience hadn't lasted long, but it was long enough to have altered me forever. When he finally pulled back and looked into my eyes, I saw the same sense of wonder and excitement I felt mirrored there.

"Wow," I whispered, unable to fathom everything that had just happened.

"Yeah," he said, sliding me that cocky grin. "That's a good word for it." He rolled to his side, taking me with him. A cool morning breeze wafted through an open window, kissing our sweat-slickened bodies. "Fuck," he groaned, leaning in to kiss me gently. "Meant that to last a bit longer."

"I wouldn't have survived," I admitted, giggling.

"Not sure I would have, either." He kissed me once more, then rolled out of bed. Heading straight for the bathroom, he tugged off the condom and tossed it in the waste basket, then washed himself. Getting a clean cloth, he came back to me and washed me gently, tossing the rag in the general direction of the bathroom. "I'll get that later. Right now, I wanna hold you."

I accepted his embrace eagerly, if with a little confusion. "I didn't think men liked to cuddle after sex."

"I take it your ex didn't."

Did I imagine it or did he stiffen? Carnage kept stroking my hair, but I could tell my answer mattered to him. "Honestly? Mark hated it. At first he'd hold me, but always when I asked for it, and not all that much. Like I said. He was in it for my money. I don't think he even liked sex with me." I snuggled closer, wanting to keep this afterglow as long as possible. "Lord knows I didn't like it with him."

"Little shit," Carnage said. "He's not important,

though I'll be looking into him later. Right now, I just need to get you settled into life with me. So, my next question is, do you and the boys have anything you need to get back at your old place?"

"Nothing important," I said. I made sure the boys knew to pack anything they wanted to keep in their backpacks."

"No video games or computers and shit?"

I winced. Yeah. No. "Mark hocked everything we had of value."

He continued stroking my back, but I could feel the tension ratchet up a notch in him. "He'll pay for everything he did to you and the boys, Calliope. I swear it."

"Like you said, he's not important," I said. "I'm just glad I got us all away from him. Well, glad you did. All I managed to do was get us into the hands of men I didn't know. I guess I took a huge risk."

"You did. But it was calculated. It wasn't a bad choice, Calliope. Not every MC is bad. Even some of the one-percenters have a code they follow that includes protecting women and children. You made the right choice."

"Did you mean what you said about Chase? I don't mind if he gets to know his sons. I'd encourage it, actually. But I won't give them to him without a fight. I was there for them. He wasn't."

"I meant every fuckin' word, Calliope." He stroked my cheek gently with his thumb. "I can take care of Chase. Cain will let him know how he feels on the subject. If it's the wrong advice or if I don't agree with it, I'll challenge Cain and forbid Chase from doing anything rash."

"You have that kind of pull with him?"

"I sponsored him at both ExFil and Bones. I got

him his job, then got him into this brotherhood. We've not been close for a while, but he respects me and my judgment. If nothing else, I'll beat his ass into submission."

"I'll trust you, then. Just… Carnage, don't break my heart. Or my boys'. I'd never be able to forgive you for that."

"You have my word, baby. You'll always be safe with me."

Chapter Five
Carnage

I was taking heat from my brothers, but pussy-whipped didn't begin to cover my feelings for Calliope. Her sons had begun to emulate me, down to pretending their bicycles were motorcycles and insisting they have vests. Calliope had tried to nix the vests because she couldn't afford it and had no idea how to make them, but the club came through in fine fashion. Cheetah made them vests with the emblem the other kids wore, proclaiming them Sons of Bones. Didn't matter if it was cheesy or not, Gunnar had started it, and we all thought it was great.

Gunnar had let the boys in readily enough, though there had been a small battle of wills when Theodore had insisted they let Hannah into the club as well. Gunnar said only boys were allowed, but Shadow pointed out that Venus was a girl and a member of Salvation's Bane, Bones's sister club. He also pointed out that his woman, Millie, was on her way to becoming a member of Bones. All of it bemused Calliope, and she'd just laughed, telling the boys to play nice or she'd confiscate their vests.

Theodore was growing a little more carefree, but I could tell he was watching me very carefully. Also, every time his mother laughed, he smiled. The kid was killing me.

It had been a little over a week since Calliope had come into my life, and she'd been with me nearly every day. I hadn't planned it that way, and it didn't seem like she had either, but I noticed her looking for me when I wasn't around. When she spotted me, her whole face would light up in both delight and relief. Yeah. She didn't get it yet, but I meant it when I said she was mine. The more I had her, the more I let her wrap herself around my heart, the more I knew this was the right decision.

My club delighted in her and the boys. All the kids took them into their little group, including them as if they were already a part of the family. Far as I was concerned, they were. The ol' ladies surrounded Calliope with their friendship and affection like we were already a couple, taking her shopping for herself and the boys. I knew Calliope wasn't comfortable letting them spend money on her, but they explained that the club took care of its own. That included her and her boys while they were with us.

"Levi?" Calliope smiled up at me from where she sat soaking up the sun by the pool. All the kids were at the local waterpark with a couple of the ol' ladies and my brothers. It had taken a lot to get Calliope to stay here, but Angel had worked her magic and got her to have an afternoon to herself.

"Hey, baby," I purred, knowing I was about to get a taste of my woman's sun-warmed skin. I could smell the suntan oil from here, and I was itching to bury my nose in her neck before I buried my face in her pussy. "Don't you look all relaxed in that sun? In that little bikini."

She grinned and stretched her arms over her head, thrusting her chest out. "I am relaxed. I love lying in the sun and just baking."

I sat on the lounge with her, pulling her over me as I worked my way underneath her. She giggled as she swatted at me. "Everyone will see!"

"Honey, this is a biker club. Don't you look around in the common room when we go at night? There are all kinds of people having sex. No one gives a good Goddamn if we fuck out here."

"Yeah, but the kids --"

"Are all at the waterpark. Every last one of the little fuckers. That means we can fuck in the sun, sweatin' so we glide together until we're so worked up we can't stand it any longer, to our heart's content. You think you're up for that?"

She shivered. "Oh, God..."

"Yeah, baby. I know. Now. You gonna stop me from takin' this little top off so I can suck on those perfect tits?"

"You know I'm not." She did glance around but didn't stop me from pulling the string at her back until it slid undone. I pulled the rest of it over her head and tossed it aside.

"So fuckin' beautiful," I murmured to her as I pulled her to me. Ducking my head, I latched on to one of her nipples, sucking and flicking the tip with my tongue before taking more of her breast into my mouth. She cried out, throwing her head back, her face raised to the sun. "Love the way your skin smells," I said between tonguing her. "Like heat and coconut. I want more."

I lifted her, standing and turning around. Straddled the lounge chair and laid her down gently on her back, flipping the chair's back down as I went. I pulled the strings at her hips, tugging the bottom of her bikini off her body to join the top. Then I hooked my arms around her thighs and lowered my face to her weeping cunt and feasted.

Had any woman ever tasted so delicious? More, her reactions got to me every fucking time. She always wiggled and squirmed, tunneling her fingers into my hair like she couldn't decide if she needed to shove me away or hold me tighter to her. Always she came. This time was no exception. I lapped up every drop as she screamed to the sky, forgetting her surroundings in her pleasure. I knew she'd be mortified to think anyone might have heard her, but I could fix that. As I gazed up at her in her abandon, I knew I was the luckiest man in the fucking world. Because the woman in my arms was mine.

I pulled out a condom from my jeans pocket and ripped it open. Undoing my fly, I let my dick out to my great relief. I was hard as steel, needing to fuck her. Calliope. Only Calliope.

When I rolled on the condom, I aimed my dick at her entrance, guiding myself inside. I wrapped my arms around her, holding her tight as I began moving inside her with a hard, driving rhythm.

"Levi," she gasped. I loved that she called me by my real name. No one else in the club did. Only her. It was something else special between us. An intimate tie. The pleasure I found in the arms of this young woman was mind boggling. Every time I took her, every time she surrendered to me was just one more tie weaving us together. I never wanted to let her go. And I knew in my heart I never would.

With that thought in mind, I nipped her neck sharply. She gasped.

"Levi!"

"That's it, Calliope. That's my girl. Come for me. So I can come in you."

"Levi! Yes! Do it!"

Her pussy squeezed my dick so hard, there was no way to hold off my orgasm. I roared my pleasure, loving the way she milked me, just as demanding of me as I was of her.

When I was spent, I clutched her to me tightly. "Ain't lettin' you go, Calliope. You're mine, and you'll always be mine."

"Don't say that," she whispered, her body shuddering in my arms. "I'm already so caught up in you I couldn't stand it if you left."

"Ain't leavin', and neither are you. Ain't sayin' I love you, but you've gotten under my skin and I can't let you go. Understand me, Calliope?" I said, pulling back to look her in the eyes, needing her to see I meant business. "I *won't* let you go."

Her eyes widened, and she shook her head slightly, trying to deny me. Then she swallowed. "I -- OK," she said. "But the boys come with me. We're a complete package. I'm not giving them up. Even for you."

"Never said you should. In fact, no matter what happens once Chase is here, they stay with me and you. No matter what. I'll get us through this."

Calliope nodded several times. "OK." Then she burst into tears.

* * *

Calliope

I believed Carnage. For some reason, I believed him. He was really on my side in this. I could see it in his eyes. Maybe it had been there all along and I'd been afraid to hope. But I saw it now. Sure, anything could still happen, but I chose to believe.

"Shh, shh… I've got you," he murmured. Somehow, he got us rolled over so that I lay on top, straddling him. Carnage held me tight, petting my hair and kissing my temple. I was acutely aware of my bare ass shining in the sun, but when he rested his big palm over one cheek, I decided I didn't really care.

One thing that impressed me about Carnage was his ability to handle my tears. More than once he'd managed to calm me when I was upset, and never once did he berate me or tell me to pull myself together. He simply dealt with it and gave me what I needed to regain my equilibrium. He reminded me a lot of Theodore, though I hated to admit it. Theo always tried to calm my tears. I knew he hated seeing me cry -- both the boys did. But Theo seemed to take it personally. It was what had gotten the boys in trouble with Mark this last time.

I made an effort to stop crying, but the more Carnage soothed me, the harder I cried. I guess I'd held it in too long.

Finally, he just held me tightly to him, running his hand soothingly up and down my back. He didn't speak or in any way try to get me to stop.

When I finally slowed to small hiccups every now and then, Carnage handed me a towel from beside the lounger. I tried to sit up, but he just tightened his hold on me until I relaxed back on top of him. I wiped my nose and face, trying to clean up.

"Come on," he said, standing up with me wrapped around him.

"Where're we goin?" I couldn't help but look around us, trying to make sure no one could see us.

"Swimmin'," he said before tossing me in the deep end of the pool.

I squealed just before splashing down. The next thing I knew, Carnage had stripped off and dove in after me. I raced to the other side, him hot on my heels. I ducked under, somersaulting and twisting in the water as I turned smoothly to race back to the other side. I made about three strokes before he snagged my ankle, pulling me under. Then I broke the surface, his arms securely around me as he gave me that deep chuckle that never failed to warm my heart. I couldn't help but smile.

"There's that beautiful smile me and the boys love." I could see what he was doing. Grouping himself and the boys as a unit, all of them wanting me happy.

I thought about it a moment, really thinking about the situation I found myself in. "Am I happy?" I looked up at him as if he held all my answers. Maybe he did. When he just quirked an eyebrow, I dug deep. Then I nodded slowly. "Yeah. I think I am. I'm happy." The admission felt like a huge weight had been lifted from my shoulders. I laughed as I tightened my arms around his neck. "I'm happy, Carnage," I whispered. "I have everything I've ever wanted, and I have you to thank for that."

"Ain't nothing I did, sweetheart. All I did was make sure you knew you were safe. Any man worth his salt would do that."

"You've also given me more pleasure than I ever thought possible. You've shown me how sex is supposed to be. I understand so much now."

"Hum," he said, a wicked gleam in his eye. "Maybe it's time to show you more."

My stomach did a slow roll, and I shivered. "Yes," I said, nodding my head. "I want you to show it all to me."

"All?"

I took a deep breath. I was all in with this. With Carnage. I wanted this man with everything in me. If that meant pushing my comfort zone, I was all for it. "Yes. I want you to show me everything about sex there is to know."

"Could take a very long time," he warned. "I won't start this unless I know you're willing to stay with me to learn everything I have to teach you."

"How long we talking about?"

"Could take months. Years, even. Hell, if you prove to be as adventurous as I think you are, it could take even longer than that."

My heart thudded in my chest. He was hinting at an actual relationship. But I had questions. "Just what would be involved? Carnage, I want this spelled out so there are no misunderstandings."

"First of all, what's my name."

I sucked in a breath. "I thought that was for during sex."

"It's for all the time. But only for you. Now. What's my name?"

"Levi." I breathed his name like it was my very breath. He was so larger than life, so exceptionally perfect to me I had no words to express. It wasn't that he'd given me his name when he said not many people knew it. It was that he was insisting I use it. I intended to test that, to push my bounds because it was the only way I had of claiming this man I wanted so badly.

"Good. Now. You explore this with me. No one else. You get me?"

I blinked, probably looking confused. "Who else would I explore it with?"

"Any single motherfucker in this place would love a shot at you. But you're taken. By me. Anyone tries to come at you, you shut it down."

"You're assuming they'll listen to me. Don't bikers usually take what they want?"

He shrugged. "Sure. We'll use anything we can to get a woman into our beds. But you shut it down, they'll respect your wishes. And if they don't respect my claim, I'll bust a motherfucker up."

I couldn't help myself -- I laughed and leaned in to kiss him. He threaded a hand in my hair, bunching it in his fist as he kissed me. There was nothing more I wanted to do than lose myself in that kiss. In the man. He had become very important to me and the boys in a very short time.

"I hope you see the way Theo and Bastian look at you. Those boys idolize you. Especially Theo. You know, I even caught him mimicking the way you walk the other day. Practicing as he walked back and forth, watching himself in the sliding glass door in our suite."

"That boy is very protective of you. He's gonna be a handful as he gets older. Don't expect him to miss anything."

"I know." That sobered me somewhat. "He's always been a little more reserved than Bastian, but since I took up with Mark --"

Carnage gave me a hard kiss, silencing the rest of my statement. "That's over and done with. That motherfucker's gone from your lives. You're startin' a new one. With me. Understand?"

But for how long?

"Carnage!" A woman in the smallest bikini I'd ever seen waved at him from the other side of the pool. Then she turned her head. "Lonnie! I found him! In the pool!"

I looked up and waved. "Hi." The woman didn't acknowledge me. Just shucked her bikini as she kept her focus on Carnage.

Her movements were sensual, her curves in perfect proportion. Long, blonde locks shimmered gold in the sun as she kicked aside the bottom of her suit. She dove in, swimming straight to us, inserting herself between me and Carnage. Had someone punched me in the stomach, I wasn't sure I could have hurt worse.

"Hey, baby," she purred.

"Get out of the pool, Ivana."

"But me and Lonnie wanna play."

"Play somewhere else. This is taken."

She reached out to touch Carnage, and I knew I had to say something. "Excuse me," I said, trying to be polite. I'd seen the women around here -- club girls, they were called -- and knew what this one and possibly her friend wanted. "You're interrupting."

She didn't even turn her head to acknowledge me. "Wouldn't be if you could keep a man like Carnage satisfied. But everyone knows you can't."

There was a splash as another naked woman dove into the water to swim to us. Probably Lonnie.

I looked at Carnage. He seemed to be waiting for... something. That was when I realized how much trouble I was in. Three things occurred to me. First, Carnage was testing me. Seeing what I would do. Second, I had two choices. Leave or behave like I thought these women would behave in the same situation. And lastly? The whole fucking scene hurt me like nothing I'd ever experienced, and I would never, ever put myself in the position to experience it again. Once was enough.

So I was left with two choices. Cut and run, or do battle with two women. In the water. Over a man.

"Fuck this shit," I said, turning to leave. Then one of them giggled. And I just... *snapped*.

Before I fully realized what I'd done, I snagged Ivana by the hair and pulled with all my might, unbalancing her in the water and shoving her under. Lonnie gasped, surprise on her face when I lunged for her. She was ready, though, splashing me with a faceful of water before attacking.

Before she could touch me, Carnage stepped between us, putting himself between me and the two women. "That's enough," he growled menacingly.

"It's not nearly enough," I hissed. How could I

have gone from the high of my life to cat-fighting with two club girls in the space of a few seconds? "Yeah. Fuck this shit." I swam to the side of the pool, pushing myself up on the side, acutely aware of my nakedness but refusing to be ashamed. With my head held high, I marched back to the lounger I'd claimed and wrapped myself in the towel.

"Not another step, Calliope," Carnage snapped.

I whirled around. "This arrangement you so thoughtfully dictated to me a while ago. The one where I don't go to anyone else for pleasure. Does that extend to you? Because it looks like you plan on getting your jollies off with every club girl in the place." I didn't bother to hide my anger, needing every single ounce of it to keep from crying again.

"You think I'm handing down a double standard?"

"Sure the fuck looks like it. You've got two of your little tarts all over you even now. Not even a full five minutes after you laid down the law to me!"

"I'm not fuckin' either of them, Calliope. I think you know that."

"Well, you sure as shit ain't turning them down!"

"So? You gonna run? Or you gonna stake your claim?"

"Do you want me to fight for you? Is that what this is about? Why didn't you just shut these two down from the start?"

"Not at all. I just wanted to see how serious you were."

"You saying you'd fight over me if one of the men around here came on to me the way these two did with you?"

"No. It wouldn't be a fight. I'd just kill the motherfucker and be done with it. No fighting to it."

I blinked. "Well. OK, then." I looked at the women in the water. Intently. Needing to memorize every feature I could about them. "I'm not a good shot with a gun, and I can't kill a person with my bare hands. But from this moment on, I'm carrying a knife with me. I may not kill anyone making a move on Levi, but I *will* cut a bitch. And yes. You can pass that on. Or not. Makes no difference to me." I glanced at Carnage. "Come with me back to my suite or stay with these bitches. Right now, I don't much care."

I stomped off, not waiting to see what happened with Carnage and the two women. I was horrified I'd gotten physical, but it had felt good. Like I was fighting for what I wanted. Hell, who was I kidding? That was exactly what I was doing. I realized he'd declared he'd kill anyone in the club who made a move on me and thought that probably wasn't something men said in a club like this. Maybe he was really serious. I knew I was. I was going to buy me a knife and do exactly what I promised. If that got me kicked out or locked up, I'd deal with it later. I needed Levi. The boys needed him. So I'd fight with my last breath for him.

I hadn't made it halfway across the yard when Carnage swooped me up over his shoulder.

"What are you doing? Put me down!"

"Nuh-uh." His hand came down on my ass hard enough to make me cry out and jump.

"What was that for?"

"For turnin' me the fuck on, baby."

"If you think we're having sex, you can think again. I'm mad at you!"

"So, angry sex, then. Best kind."

Judging by the way my pussy just clenched, I'd have to agree with his assessment.

Chapter Six
Carnage

Sleeping with Calliope in my arms had to be the best feeling in the whole world. I went to sleep with her scent surrounding me every single night. My need for her proved to be greater than any time in my entire life. Sometimes I'd fuck her two or three times in the night. And it wasn't all me. She was just as possessive and needy of my attentions as I was of hers.

She hadn't been bluffing when she'd said she was going to carry a knife, either. Somehow, the woman had found the biggest Bowie knife I'd ever seen and had taken to wearing it at her hip. More than once she'd fingered that knife when Ivana had approached me. There was always a gleam in her eyes like she was just wishing the bitch would. Whenever that happened, she'd find herself over my shoulder on the way back to our room for a hard, wild fuck.

Now, I lay in bed with her, lazily petting her back while she slept. It soothed me on some level to touch her like this. Just… up and down with my hand on her arm or back while she slept. More than one of my brothers had snickered and called me pussy-whipped, but I didn't care. Hell, I freely admitted it.

Just as I was dozing off, my phone buzzed in my pocket. Text message. Of course, it was from Chase. Fuck. He wasn't due back for another few days, and I'd been glad of it. Once he was back, there was a whole other can of worms to delve into. Sure, Cain had probably sent word he was needed back, but those orders were usually secondary to whatever mission his men were on.

Chase: *Cain's called me back early. Problem?*
How to answer that?

Me: *Maybe. He didn't tell you what was going on?*

Chase: *Wouldn't be asking you if he had. What you hiding?*

Of course, the younger man would know I was stalling. But what to tell him?

Me: *Where you at now?*

Chase: *On a plane back to Somerset.*

Me: *How you using your phone on a plane?*

Chase: *Private plane, dumbass. Be there in thirty.*

Kid was feeling out what he was stepping into. I debated on whether or not to tell him. I'd sponsored Chase when he'd first applied to work at ExFil, and again when he'd wanted to prospect for Bones. He'd been with a mercenary outfit taking questionable orders from questionable people. He'd stood up for what was right, refusing a kill order without first going through the proper protocol to verify it. It had impressed everyone in Bones. Especially Data, since it was his woman Chase had been ordered to kill. We'd been pretty close three or four years ago, but he had a life of his own. We were MC brothers, but not close friends. Likely he'd reached out to me because of our past ties. Force of habit.

Me: *Do you remember a woman named Cherry Mills?*

There was a long pause. So long, I thought he might have set his phone down.

Chase: *She and I were together for several months when I was prospecting for Bones. When you guys sent me to Salvation's Bane to work with Red at the garage. She looking for me?*

So, Chase was totally in the dark. About everything. I wasn't sure what to feel or who to be angry at. In any case, this wasn't a conversation to have via text.

Very carefully, I extracted myself from Calliope's

arms and stood, covering her carefully and leaving the room. Then I called Chase.

"I haven't seen or heard from Cherry in nine or ten years," Chase said by way of greeting. "What's she doing there? How'd she find me?"

"She ain't. When was the last time you spoke to her?"

There was silence while I imagined Chase thought it over. "The night I left. She and her little sister were giving me grief about the club. Neither of them could believe Bones or Bane were any better than gangs. Cherry was pretty hardcore against it while her sister went along for the ride. Callie was her name. Why? I mean, hell. I'd be glad to see her. Cherry wasn't a bad person. Just… I don't know. Young?" He snorted. "Seems stupid to say because she was a year older than me."

"So you had no contact with her, or anyone representing her, after you left?"

"Carnage, what's going on?"

I sighed, scrubbing a hand over my face. "We'll talk when you get here. This is something you need to see for yourself. Besides, if Cain didn't tell you, I'm not going to overstep."

"This going to affect my standing with the club?"

I thought about that. Would it? "Depends, I guess. I'd say if you just tell the truth, everything will be fine. Did you mistreat Cherry in any way?"

"Hell, no! How could you even ask me that? I've done some questionable things, but I've never harmed an innocent woman. Certainly never one I was involved with!"

"All right, all right. I'm not accusing you, Chase, and no one else is."

"Fuck. What was I supposed to do? Stay when

she clearly didn't want me there? What's she saying about me? I only left because she gave me an ultimatum. Her or the club. And we'd only been together a month. I didn't love her. She didn't love me."

"Just get here. We'll sort this out then."

"Don't like going in blind, Carnage."

"Then you'll just have to trust your brothers. Cain's always going to let you have your say. And this has nothing to do with the club. As long as you didn't abuse Cherry or her sister, you're good with the club."

Chase sounded tired when he sighed. "Fine. Who's coming to get me?"

"I think Cain sent Tool. He'll be in the Bronco."

"Roger that. I'll see you when we get there." He ended the call.

I'd have to wake Calliope soon. But not yet. Cain would text when he was ready. In the meantime, I went back to her, sliding into the bed next to her. Calliope wiggled closer until she had her head on my shoulder and was clutching my shirt once again. Yeah. I was so fucked. This woman was so under my skin I was never going to get her out. Wasn't sure I even wanted to. I meant what I'd promised her almost from the start. I would protect her right to those boys with my last breath. If that meant going against my brothers or my president, I'd do it gladly.

Fifteen minutes later, I got the text from Cain I'd been expecting and dreading.

Come to church. Bring Calliope.

What about boys?

No. You and Calliope can introduce them to Chase tomorrow.

It was still early, but not too early. The sun was rising over the mountain on what promised to be another beautiful day. The boys would probably still be asleep in their room, but I always locked the door to our room so they didn't walk in on anything inappropriate. Much as I hated doing this, the sooner we got it over with, the better I'd feel. Also, I knew it was time to claim my woman irrevocably.

I kissed my way down Calliope's naked body, sucking each nipple gently and laving the peak. She moved restlessly but didn't wake, moaning softly in her sleep. By the time I got to her sweet pussy, she was gasping with need.

"Levi!" Her cry was loud and sounded slightly confused. I watched her intently as she fell apart, her expression unfocused at first before she found my gaze with hers and locked on. "Oh, wow." One hand flew to my head, and I chuckled against her clit, giving it one final swipe before rubbing my face against her thigh and crawling up her body to cover her.

"Are you ready for me, sweet Calliope? I'm takin' you bareback this time. You good with that?"

Her eyes widened. "I -- I've never..."

"Me neither." That admission didn't cost me the way I thought it might. Instead, it felt like a promise. Like I was admitting to her exactly what I was doing. That this was forever and not just a few months or even a couple of years. This was as close as I could come to asking -- no, demanding -- for her forever. And I felt *right*.

"I'm not... that is, I'm not on birth control."

Before I realized I'd done it, I grinned at her. Fuck it. "*Good.*" Then I slid into her hot wetness in a smooth glide.

At once I was swamped with sensations. I was the experienced one, but I had none with this. Being inside Calliope raw was an awakening. As if all I'd ever done was straight fucking, then suddenly discovered there was a whole new world of kinky, dirty things a man and woman could do together. No way I was lasting long like this.

Calliope clung to me. "So hot," she gasped. "Holy shit!"

"Unh!" I grunted as I surged into her. The longer I fucked her, the more of myself I gave her. Too late, I realized my mistake. I'd never believed in instant love. Life just sucked too hard for that. But having such an intimate connection with this girl took what little I had left to give of my heart and carved out the rest to add to it and give to Calliope on a silver fucking platter. I. Was. Done.

With a hard-driving surge, I fucked Callipe. Harder. Faster. I did my best to put the friction she needed on her clit, but rational thought was a dim haze in the back of my mind I couldn't seem to access.

I wrapped my arms around her tightly, holding her to me as I fucked her. My face was buried in the side of her neck, and my whole world narrowed to the pleasure currently engulfing my fucking dick. "Fuck! Fuck! Fuck!" I groaned my orgasm, my mouth muffled by her neck. Calliope stiffened around me, her cunt gripping my cock in a pulsing caress. Then she screamed. Violently.

Turning her face to me, I kissed her, doing my best to capture her screams so she didn't wake the kids. Her pussy continued to pulse and grip me like a tight fist, taking every drop of my seed deep into her tender body. I wanted to howl at the moon. Fuck! I guess I had when I came. Before, if I'd even thought I'd accidentally come inside a woman, I'd have panicked. There had never been a time in my life when I'd fucked a woman I wanted to keep for longer than the pleasure lasted. Calliope? Yeah. I'd known she was a keeper from the very beginning.

We lay there, neither of us moving, for a long time. I knew I had to be heavy, but she just lay beneath me, stroking my back like she was petting a big jungle cat. Her other hand was at my nape, her fingers massaging gently. If there was ever anything that felt better than this, I couldn't fathom what it might be. This woman was going to be my everything. She and her boys had exploded into my life, and I'd protect and defend them to the fucking death.

* * *

Calliope

I wasn't sure how I felt about what I'd just allowed to happen. I mean, what was next for me and Carnage? I was sure he'd always be there for his kid, but would he stay with me? What if I had to see him with other women when he left me? Because I couldn't go far if I were pregnant. I knew enough to know Carnage would never allow it.

Not wanting to push the situation or draw attention to myself, I lay passively beneath Carnage. It wasn't a hardship, because I loved being pinned beneath him.

"I hate to bring this up, but we've got to go to church."

"Church?" That was odd. "I don't have a dress, Carnage. I can't --"

He kissed me and chuckled. "Church is where the club meets, honey. Just a segregated part of the clubhouse. Usually, only members are allowed in, but Cain wants you there."

"That doesn't sound good." I got a foreboding feeling in my chest.

"No worries for you, baby. I'll take care of everything." He smoothed my hair away from my face and kissed me gently. "Chase is here. Cain wants this settled now."

My breath caught and I felt like my chest was going to explode. "I -- I…"

"Shh, baby. Everything's gonna be all right." Carnage continued to kiss me. He kissed my eyes and cleaned my tears when a few leaked to streak down my temples. "Trust me, baby. I swear I won't let anything happen to take the boys away from you." He rolled us over and kept me close, petting me gently.

I couldn't say anything. All I could do was nod. Carnage and his crew had gotten me and the boys out of a bad situation. Surely, they wouldn't betray me in that kind of way. "Just, please don't anyone tear us apart, Levi," I said, my voice breaking. "I can't have those boys taken from me."

"And they wouldn't want to be taken from you, either, honey. They love you. That's all I need to know. Just trust me. Don't talk unless I give you the OK. Don't pay attention to anyone but me. You look to me. Always."

"OK." I nodded eagerly. I'd do anything he said if he promised to make this right.

We dressed, Carnage helping me when I dragged my feet. He didn't say anything mean or get impatient with me. He just leveled his steady gaze on me and nodded encouragingly.

"Come on," he said. "Keep your head up. You've got nothing to worry about or apologize for, no matter what anyone says."

"They think I've done something wrong?" Oh, God! Just how much trouble was I in?

"Nope. I just don't know how Chase will react.

None of this is your fault. You were the one who kept those boys safe. My guess is he'll be angry at himself and will try to take it out on you. I will *always* stand between you and everyone. Physically and verbally. He's not going to berate you under any circumstances. So, I'm going to ask you this one time just to know what I'm walking into. Not as an accusation or because I believe you did anything wrong. Just for informational purposes. Is there anything you need to tell me about you or your sister's relationship with Chase that you haven't?"

"No. I told you everything I knew. Like I said, they fought a lot, but I wasn't a part of that." My heart was pounding, and my knees were weak. I wasn't sure I could get up and walk anywhere in that moment.

Carnage knelt in front of me where I sat on the bed. He took my hands in his, kissing my knuckles. "Trust me, Calliope. Just… trust me. I'll take care of all of you."

"I know," I said, finding I actually meant it. I did trust him. With everything. "I'm just scared." I sniffed, closing my eyes and taking a deep, calming breath. When I opened them, I looked directly at him. "I know. I trust you."

"Good," he said, standing and framing my face as he kissed me gently. "Let's go. The sooner this is over the better you'll feel."

My hand firmly in his, Carnage walked me to their meeting room. Church, as he called it. Chase was there, quietly talking to Data, the club's computer guy. I'd met him several times along with his wife, Zora. I really liked them both, but would they be with me or against me on this? Cain sat in the middle of a curved table, talking quietly with Bohannon, the enforcer of the club. I tried to keep my head up, but it was fucking hard. I was scared out of my mind. The only thing that kept me on my feet when I saw Chase was Carnage's firm grip on my hand.

"Take a breath, baby. You're fine."

All I could do was nod. My eyes were on Chase while he continued to talk to Data. A couple of times he shook his head or said something short. He looked hard, but not angry. Then he glanced over and caught my gaze. He did a double take, then gave me a cordial nod, lifting one side of his mouth in a half grin. He didn't look like a man who was out to get me or take my boys. Looks could be deceiving, though.

"Carnage," Cain called out. He didn't raise his voice, but everyone in the room stopped talking. Carnage nodded at Cain and tugged me with him to stand in front of a chair in front of the table. My heart sank

"Am I on trial?" My voice wavered as I looked up at Carnage.

"No, honey."

"We just have some questions for both you and Chase," Cain said. I remembered how horrible he was the first time I'd met him. He was the president of this club. There was no way he was going to take my side if Chase wanted his kids. It took everything in me to not panic.

"It's OK, Calliope," Carnage murmured, his hand on my shoulder. "I'm here. I'm not going anywhere. I'm not lettin' anyone take your children. Keep that foremost in your mind." All I could do was nod and breathe.

Cain turned to Chase. "How was your flight, brother?" It was everything I could do not to sob openly. I clenched my fists and tried to stay sane, because it was obvious who the outsider was here.

And it wasn't Chase.

"Long. Why'd you call me back early? What's going on?" He glanced at me, but still addressed Cain. "Is Calliope OK?"

Cain lifted an eyebrow at me. As instructed, I looked at Carnage for instructions. When he nodded, I answered softly, "I'm fine."

"Where's Cherry?" Chase asked. "You guys were always together."

I swallowed and glanced at Carnage again. He squeezed my shoulder and nodded again. Taking a deep breath, I said, "She's dead."

Chase looked like I'd punched him. He actually took a step backward, shaking his head. He cleared his throat. "How?"

"Cancer," I answered. "Didn't you hear from her lawyer?"

Carnage squeezed my shoulder until I looked at him, then shook his head. *Ease up*. I got it.

"I -- No. Like I told Carnage earlier, I haven't heard from Cherry since the day I left. What the fuck is going on, Cain?" Chase was losing his patience. "You called me in early and no one" -- he whirled around to pin Carnage with a hard stare --"not my brothers or my friends, will tell me fuckin' why. This is my life, and I won't be kept in the fuckin' dark any longer!"

Carnage sighed. "Chase, Calliope adopted and raised Cherry's twin boys. She had them less than a year after you left, and Calliope says Cherry told her you were their father."

I clenched my fists, holding myself as still as I could. If possible, Chase looked even more agitated. "*I'm* the father?"

"That's what she told me," I said softly before I remembered I wasn't supposed to say anything.

Chase pinned me with his gaze, and I dropped my head, very much intimidated. "Calliope, I'm not sure what exactly Cherry told you, but I can assure you I'm not the father of any of her children."

I sucked in a breath. "But… but she told me. She said she had her lawyer try to find you in case you wanted them. She tried to make sure you were in the loop and had every opportunity to be with your children if you wanted it."

As he looked at me, I could see confusion on his face. "What's all this about? Did I do something to hurt you or Cherry? Carnage told me to tell the truth, but I'm not sure what the question here is."

"If Calliope has your children, Chase, we need to discuss how much, if any, involvement you want to have in their lives," Cain explained. "You should know that Calliope adopted those boys at birth and has raised them as her own."

"Wait," Chase said, waving me away like I'd been the one to speak. "You're telling me that at sixteen, you, a minor, adopted your sister's children?"

"Well, I was seventeen by the time they were born, but I was emancipated. I had my GED and was working a full-time job. We were poor kids. Kids nobody wanted. With the help of Cherry's lawyer, I got custody instead of the boys going into foster care. Since Cherry had custody of me before her lawyer helped me get emancipated, all three of us would have had to go into foster care. The way the judge saw it, by giving me, their closest relative, custody, it saved the state money. I was self-sufficient with a job of my own, out of school, and practically begging to keep the kids. So, yeah. I kept my sister's children and raised them as my own. I adopted them so it was all legal. The only question was you. Which was why the lawyer tried to find you. Cherry told me she told you she was pregnant before you left. She said her lawyer tried to find you after the boys were gone. I honestly didn't care, because I had bigger problems at the time."

Chase sighed and sat heavily in a nearby chair, scrubbing a hand over his face. He seemed to be weighing what he needed to say, but he didn't look at Cain or Carnage. He kept this between the two of us.

"Callie, your sister did tell me she was pregnant before she left. She told me I was the father. But there was no way I could have been the father of those boys. I always, *always*, used a condom. Also, to erase any doubt, I gave blood for a paternity test when she was about ten weeks along. Once the negative test came back" -- he shrugged --"I left. There was nothing left to talk about at that point. She'd been unfaithful for whatever reason and gotten pregnant. What was I supposed to do?"

I nearly lost it then. Tears leaked from my eyes, but I managed to hold it to just a couple. "So you're not the boys' father?"

"If there had been any question, I'd have stayed. Hell, had I known she had cancer, I'd have come back to make sure she was taken care of. Understand me, I didn't love her, but I could have. I certainly would have made sure she had peace of mind about her children, even if they weren't mine."

"Did you change your phone number after you left? She said you had. That her lawyer got a disconnected number."

"No, Callie. I have the same cell number I've always had. If she'd wanted to get a hold of me, she could have."

Since our mother's death, my life had been a desperate struggle to just survive. There had been moments of joy, but mostly it had been struggle, pain, and fear. Now, for the first time in longer than I could remember, I felt hope blooming in my chest.

I looked up at Carnage, needing reassurance from him. Needed it with all my might. "So I get to keep my boys?" My voice broke when I asked the question.

"You thought I'd take two kids away from the person who's been with them since their birth?" Chase sounded horrified.

"I thought they were your kids," I said, the tears coming now in an uncontrollable flood. "I thought you might want custody after you found out their mom was dead since you never had the choice."

"Honey. Callie. If they'd been mine, I'd want to be a part of their lives. I'd help you any way I could. But I'd never just… *take them*. You were just as special to me as Cherry was, just in a different way. Like a little sister I adored. So, I'll still help you, honey. Any way I can. But I'll never hurt you or your kids. Never."

I reached for Carnage, and he lifted me into his arms and I just lost it. I cried so hard I couldn't process anything else around me other than Carnage's strong arms and the wide chest I sobbed into.

I'm not really sure what happened after that. I vaguely remember hearing Carnage asking if we were done before we left. The next thing I really registered was Carnage laying me down on our bed and pulling me into his arms, comforting me. Telling me how it was all done. It was over. The boys were mine and his. He'd never leave us alone. We'd always have someone protecting us.

I believed him.

Chapter Seven
Calliope

"I can't believe you guys bought a late show at the movie theater." The ol' ladies of the club -- all ten of them -- had paid the local theater for a late-night party for the newest blockbuster the night *before* it was to have an early showing. They'd all invited a few friends outside the club, and I was invited, too. Super-sized girls' night out. Angel seemed to be the organizer of the party.

"We don't do it often, but we've got a good relationship with a few business owners in the community, and we pay them well for stuff like this." She grinned, looking pleased with herself.

"This is so cool! We'll be the first ones to see this!"

"Yep. But it's probably outside whatever contract they have with the movie studios to show the movie any earlier than strictly specified, so you can't say anything or they won't let us do it again."

"Completely understandable." I grinned. "You guys are so cool."

Angel hugged me. "Of course, we are."

The only men in the area were men who worked for the cinema. They were all strictly professional, most of them being quite young. With all the stunning women in the Bones party, I was surprised those women didn't get hit on, but, though everyone was friendly, no one crossed that line.

Two guys stuck out. One was the manager. I knew this from pictures of the staff on the wall I'd looked at while we waited for the last show to end before we were escorted to our theater.

The second was the only one who seemed to be

older than the rest. Older being out of his late teens or early twenties. I put his age at somewhere between thirty-five and forty. It was hard to tell. He looked like he'd had a hard life but wasn't as old as he appeared. Drugs? Alcohol? Wasn't my business. But something about him seemed… off. More than once I caught him staring at me. I wasn't a coward, but I was in a strange town with people I barely knew, so I decided it was prudent to stick close to the people I did know. And this was the first time I'd been outside the Bones compound without Carnage at my side.

"Rain?" I sidled up to a dark-haired woman. She was married to Arkham and a fierce fighter in her own right. She was short and petite but had a hard look in her eyes sometimes.

She gave me a warm smile. "You want to sit with me?"

"Yeah. I'd like that." I returned her smile, and she looped her arm through mine. "Just a quick question. Do you know that guy standing next to the exit? He's been staring at me, and it's a little unnerving."

She glanced in the direction I indicated but had a confused look on her face. "What guy?"

I looked and he was gone. "I -- I'm not… he was there just a minute ago."

She shrugged but frowned as she glanced around us. The woman was incredibly aware of her surroundings most times. "I don't see anyone here I don't recognize, but that's not to say I didn't miss someone." By the way she continued to look even when her first impression had been that all was clear, I could tell she was taking me seriously. Which made me feel infinitely better. "I'll text Arkham, just in case. He and the boys always patrol the area on girls' night out, anyway." She shook her head and frowned as she shot off a text. "I'd love to say they did it just to annoy us, but I know it's because they're all so overprotective it's ridiculous."

It wasn't long before Arkham and Torpedo, the vice president, appeared at the entrance to our theater, Torpedo speaking into a microphone at his wrist. Both men scanned the area before nodding to Rain and me. Then they backed out.

"Guess it was just my imagination," I gave a half-hearted laugh and ducked my head.

"Hey," Rain said, grabbing my hand and squeezing. "If there's one thing I learned before I came to Bones, it's to trust your gut. Nothing's unimportant if it makes you uncomfortable." She retained possession of my hand and marched to the top of the steps in the stadium seating at the back of the theater and put us in the middle of the back row. We could see everything fine with no chance of someone sneaking up behind us.

I gave her a relieved smile. "Thanks so much, Rain."

"What are sisters for if not to have your back?"

Sisters. If I was with Carnage and he was with his club brothers, I guess that did make all the ol' ladies my sisters. The thought filled me with happiness. I didn't have to be alone anymore. I'd witnessed how all the ol' ladies had pitched in to help with each other's children. And the kids were like one big family. As far as they were concerned, they were all brothers and sisters together. I wanted that for Theo and Bastian, could already see it in their forming relationships with the other children of Bones.

With a grin, I turned to Rain. "Thank you so much. All of you have been so wonderful with me and the boys."

She smiled warmly. "You're welcome. I'm glad you found Carnage. He's a good man. A strong fighter and protector. He'll do right by you and your boys."

"He already has." Emotion threatened to overwhelm me as I thought about all Carnage had brought into my life. He was wrong about himself. He wasn't trouble. He was the best man I'd ever met.

He was also a good judge of his brothers. Chase was a good man. Better than I'd ever realized. He had, indeed, taken to my sons, teaching them and giving them another strong role model to emulate. I'd never really shared my sister's opinion of Chase's club, but I'd gone along with her because she was my older sister as well as my guardian. I could see now just exactly how wrong she'd been.

The movie was as awesome as predicted, and the girls were rambunctious, whooping and hollering when one good-looking guy after another in the movie took off his shirt or played sports until his muscled physique was glistening with sweat. At the end, they all cheered and clapped in robust, biker fashion. It was the best theater experience of my life.

"So," Rain said, looping her arm through mine as we walked outside. "How did you like your first girls' night out?"

"That was excellent!"

"Good!" She squeezed my arm. "But the night's not over. We're going to the Boneyard next for drinks and dancing. The guys will probably join us because they're territorial and all, but it's still a great time."

I was about to respond when I noticed Rain's eyes widen. Her mouth opened as if she intended to say something just before I was yanked backward and nearly pulled off my feet. I gave a sharp cry. Then I felt the cold, sharp sting of a knife at my throat.

My world narrowed to the arm across my chest and the knife against my skin. I thought I heard a woman crying out. Rain? Then the roar of several men and the sound of boots hurrying in our direction and men yelling.

"You stay put, bitch," the man at my back ordered. Foul breath feathered over my cheek, making me retch. "I know you got money. Mark said you did."

"He took everything I had."

"Maybe. But you took up with this lot, and word is they got money. I want a bunch of it."

"I can't get you money! It's not mine!"

"No, but them bastard kids are mine." He chuckled. "I'll just go to the fuckin' courts and tell 'em, and you'll have to pay me somethin' for takin' my fuckin' kids."

"I don't even know who you are!"

"I'm your bitch of a sister's supplier," he said gleefully, as if he enjoyed tearing my heart out. "She moved drugs for me."

"Cherry didn't sell drugs! Are you out of your mind?"

"'Course she did," he scoffed. "For over two years. She lasted longer than most bitches 'cause she didn't use." He chuckled. "Until she did. After that, I had her any time I wanted her, and all it cost me was a little bit of smack."

"Are... are you saying you're the father of her children?" My voice trembled, and I just couldn't wrap my mind around what he was saying.

"Yep. She even had one of those DNA tests done on me. Proves I'm their daddy."

"You never came to the hospital," I said, fear still gripping me, but now anger threatened to overtake it all. "Why are you here? Huh? Why are you doing this? The boys are taken care of, and you'll never get your filthy hands on them!"

"If you wanna live, you'll give 'em to me. Mark and I had a deal. I'd get rid of the brats for him, and he could do whatever he wanted with you."

"Get rid of? You mean you were going to kill them?"

"Hell, no!" He barked out a short laugh. "Gonna sell the brats. Get me a good price, and I'll have enough money for anything I want. After I pay Mark in his favorite currency. Cocaine."

"You're not selling my kids!" I yelled at him and started struggling. He wasn't a big man or overly muscular, but he was still strong. The knife dug into my flesh, and I felt a trickle of blood.

"Let her go now, and I promise you a clean death."

Carnage!

My relief was so overwhelming I nearly sobbed. My eyes found him unerringly. He stood there, his dreadlocks free and snapping about his head in a sudden wind. In his hand was a hatchet he twirled in his palm as if readying himself to attack.

"I ain't the one dyin', you motherfucker. It's this bitch. Now, where are my brats?"

"This is your last chance," Carnage said, turning his head. "Let her go, and it ends swiftly."

The guy ducked behind me, pulling me to one side so he could get a better grip on me. He pointed at Carnage with his knife. "I'm gonna slit the bitch's throat right in front of you. You can have the pleasure of watchin' her die, motherfucker!"

Almost faster than I could blink, Carnage threw the hatchet. It sank into the guy's thigh with a sickening thud. The one he'd left exposed when he shifted me to his right side. I darted underneath his arm and straight for Carnage. He met me with one arm open, the other pulling his gun to aim at the guy now writhing on the ground.

"Put him in the cage." Torpedo snapped out his command just as someone -- I couldn't tell who in the dark -- yanked out the hatchet, to the guy's sharp yelp, and handed it to Carnage. "Take him to the barn."

"The b-barn?" I looked up at Carnage. His mien was vicious. Like he was itching to take this guy apart.

"It's where we take people for… enhanced interrogation." Carnage imparted the knowledge looking at the man. Not at me.

"It's not spoken about," Rain said softly. Then raising her voice slightly, she added, "People who go there for questioning don't come back."

Just as the guy started to scream his protest, someone slapped a strip of duct tape over his mouth and wound it around his head three or four times. They definitely had no plans to let him loose anytime soon.

I shivered and turned into Carnage who immediately pushed me to arm's length, gripping my chin in his hand and tilting my head back.

"He cut you?"

"I -- I don -- I don't know." I shivered, the adrenaline rush starting to crash.

"Someone get me a flashlight."

Rain came up beside me, stroking my hair and shining a light from her phone on my neck. "She's got a nick," she said. "Nothing horrible. Just a small trickle of blood. She's fine, Carnage. She's fine." Rain sounded almost as shaken up as I felt.

"Motherfucker," Carnage muttered, then turned

and kicked the guy in the gut. "Get this piece of shit outta here," he snapped.

"You get first shot at him," Torpedo said. "We got his ID. Data will have info on him shortly. Got a feelin' this one needs killin' sooner rather than later."

"Just find out who he'd planned on sellin' our kids to. We'll take out both motherfuckers."

"Always the plan, brother," Torpedo said, giving Carnage a look.

"Calm down, Levi," I said softly into his neck as he held me close. "I'm not well versed in the MC culture, but I'm pretty sure Torpedo outranks you." I heard Torpedo snort before he clapped Carnage on the back.

"Yeah," Carnage said with a sigh. "But it wasn't his woman who had a knife held to her throat. I'm not going to get over that anytime soon."

"Just… can we not tell the boys?"

"Hadn't planned on it, but you know they'll find out."

"OK, so how about just not tonight?"

"Good plan." Carnage scooped me up and carried me to his bike. "Let's get home so I can look you over."

* * *

Carnage

It took every ounce of strength I possessed to make the fucking ride home and not take Calliope to the fucking Emergency Room. The *only* reason I didn't was that Mama and Pops were back from Florida. Mama was our club doctor, and she could give Calliope an exam and tell me if she needed stitches or psychiatric counseling or if there was anything else wrong with her.

"Someone have Mama meet us in her clinic," I radioed the group.

"Copy." That was Torpedo. Likely, I'd pay for my breach of protocol, as Calliope pointed out, but I didn't give a fuck at this point.

When we got home, I took Calliope into Mama's clinic. The older woman fussed over Calliope appropriately while I sat in a chair by the exam table trembling like a newborn fucking baby.

"I think your man there is in worse shape than you are, dear." Mama patted Calliope's knee before dabbing some peroxide on the wound at her neck. Mama called it a scratch, but all I saw was a gaping wound on my woman's neck. Mama didn't treat it lightly, though. She cleaned it, put ointment on it, bandaged it, then gave Calliope a tetanus shot for good measure. "Maybe a little vitamin V for you, Carnage?"

"Vitamin V? What the fuck is that?"

"Valium," Mama deadpanned. Calliope giggled. I gave the girl a warning glance, but I couldn't help it when my lips twitched. "That's what I thought," Mama said. "Now, you make sure she knows how you feel."

"Christ, Mama. She already knows I think she hung the fuckin' moon."

"Right. But does she know you love her?"

Calliope gasped, turning to look at me. "You never said that."

I opened my mouth, and shut it again.

"You *never* said that!"

"Well," Mama said, cleaning up after herself with snappish movements, obviously displeased I hadn't properly shared my feelings with Calliope. "Perhaps you should remedy that ASAP."

Right. I scrubbed my hand over the back of my

neck. "Now isn't exactly the time I'd have picked for this," I said, glancing at Calliope.

"Levi?"

"Look," I said, readying myself to go into my pitch. "You and the boys need someone to take care of you. Theodore told me that the first night we met. I already told you we were together. So I thought we should make it official. You'll marry me, and I'll adopt the boys, too." It wasn't bad as proposals went, I thought.

Mama snorted. Calliope looked at me in confusion. "You want…" She shook her head. "You want to marry me?"

"Men." Mama rolled her eyes.

"Well, yeah. It's not a difficult decision to make. You need me. I'll be your protector."

"But… what do *you* need? You'd grow to resent us after a while. Is marriage the best thing? I mean, you can protect us without tying your life to ours."

"Sweet Jesus in the manger," Mama said. "Calliope, when this moron finally tells you what you need to hear, I'll be an old, old woman. Let me know if you need my help to bash some sense into the bastard." She glanced at me, then left me and Calliope alone.

I didn't take my eyes off Calliope. She seemed to be considering everything that had happened over the last few weeks. "You said I was yours and you were mine. That neither of us would go to anyone else for relief. For sex. But…" She looked up at me, tears swimming in her eyes as she did. "Why? Why did you want that?"

"I --" I cleared my throat. "Because…"

"Levi?" She whispered my name. A plea.

I closed my eyes. And saw her with that fucking

knife to her throat. *I'm gonna slit the bitch's throat right in front of you.* Sweat broke out on my brow, and my breath came in shallow pants. "I can't lose you, Calliope," I croaked. "I fuckin' can't!"

"Look. I'm gonna tell you something," she said, standing from the exam table and crossing to stand between my legs. "I think you know it, but I'm going to say it anyway. Levi, I love you." I sucked in a breath. "More than I ever thought possible in such a short time. But you made me fall in love with you because of the way you treated me and the boys. From the very beginning you were the man we all needed. So, yeah. I love you. I'll marry you if that's what you tell me to do, because it's what I want. With all my heart. But…" She sniffed, brushing away a tear that strayed down her cheek. "I don't want to do something that will ultimately make you miserable."

"You're fuckin' killin' me, Calliope," I said, pulling her to me. I wrapped my arms around her body and buried my face in her belly. She stroked my hair, clutching me to her the same as I clutched her to me. "When I saw that knife…" I couldn't catch my breath. "Calliope…"

"Oh, Levi." She straddled my lap and wrapped herself around me. "You do love me, don't you?"

"Calliope. My Calliope."

"Yes, Levi. I'm yours. You're mine."

"I'm yours," I gasped out. "You're mine."

Then I started tugging at her clothing. Mama had looked her over, but I needed more. I need to see every inch of her body. Then I needed to lose myself in her.

"You hurt anywhere?"

"Yes," she gasped. "I hurt here," she pulled my hand between her legs. "I ache!"

"Motherfuck," I bit out. "Gonna fuck you,

Calliope. Doin' it and makin' you mine."

She cupped my face in her hands. "I'm already yours, Levi. I have been since that first day, and I think you know it."

I managed to get my dick out of my pants and slid myself inside her. We both groaned, but Calliope didn't wait for me to take over this time. She moved on me, rocking her hips in a steady roll.

"I love you, Levi. Carnage. I love you. I love you!"

"I love you, too, Calliope. So fuckin' much!"

Then I let Calliope take me to oblivion. When I came, it was with Calliope coming apart in my arms, her pussy gripping me, taking my seed from me in an almost violent fashion.

When it was over, I held her tightly, rocking her gently. I felt more grounded. Like she was real. Safe.

Safe.

"I didn't hurt you, did I?" I kissed her neck. Her ear. Her temple.

"No, Levi," she said softly, her breath still a little ragged. "You could never hurt me."

"Not intentionally, baby. Fuck!" I couldn't process everything I was feeling. "I almost lost you, Calliope."

She wrapped her naked body around my fully clothed one. "But you didn't. You saved me."

"I'll always come for you. Always."

"I know. Where're the boys?"

"Sleepover with Cain and Angel's kids. I doubt they even know there's a problem."

"Good. Take me to our room," she said. "Take me there and hold me. Everything will feel better tomorrow."

I did as she asked, wrapping a blanket around

her and carrying her to our room. Once there, I stripped and climbed into bed with Calliope and just held her for a long, long time. She held me as close as I held her. I wasn't sure I'd ever be comfortable being separated from her again, but I'd think about that later. She was here with me now. In my arms.

"What's going to happen to that man?" I'd been dreading this question. She knew but giving her the truth was still hard.

"You know, Callie. We can't let him get away with selling children. We have to find out if he was just spouting nonsense, or if he really had a buyer for… if he had a buyer."

"And if he did?"

"Then we'll find out who it was and how to find him. And we'll get rid of him."

"What about Mark?" She sounded like it was more an afterthought than anything else, but she had to ask.

"We've already got Data and Zora working on finding him. I don't think he'll come after you. Probably was too high to have any idea where to start. But we're not taking chances. We'll find him."

"And then?"

I shrugged. "Do you want to know, Calliope? Because I won't lie to you."

"I never want you to lie to me, Levi. But you don't have to answer. I know you're going to get rid of him, too."

"He deserves it for hitting you. But with all the other things he did, for planning to sell your children for drugs… Yeah. I'll take great pleasure in ending him."

"I suppose I should be upset about that, but I'm not. He does deserve it."

"What about us?" I asked. "You good to stay with me? To marry me? Be my ol' lady?"

She smiled and leaned in to kiss me. "There's nothing more I want than for us all to be a family, Levi. If that's what you're offering, then I'll grab on with both hands."

"That's what I'm offering, baby. You and the boys will always be mine. We'll have our little family, then the big extended one. The boys will have a safe place to grow up and men to teach them how to be men. You will always have me. As long as I live, I'll love you."

"There's nothing more I can ask for."

"Then it's settled."

"It is." She sighed and cuddled me closer. "I love you, Levi. Forever."

"Love you, too, baby. Always."

And I knew I always would.

Marteeka Karland

Erotic romance author by night, emergency room tech/clerk by day, Marteeka Karland works really hard to drive everyone in her life completely and totally nuts. She has been creating stories from her warped imagination since she was in the third grade. Her love of writing blossomed throughout her teenage years until it developed into the totally unorthodox and irreverent style her English teachers tried so hard to rid her of.

Marteeka at Changeling: changelingpress.com/marteeka-karland-a-39

Changeling Press E-Books

More Sci-Fi, Fantasy, Paranormal, and BDSM adventures available in e-book format for immediate download at ChangelingPress.com -- Werewolves, Vampires, Dragons, Shapeshifters and more -- Erotic Tales from the edge of your imagination.

What are E-Books?

E-books, or electronic books, are books designed to be read in digital format -- on your desktop or laptop computer, notebook, tablet, Smart Phone, or any electronic e-book reader.

Where can I get Changeling Press E-Books?

Changeling Press e-books are available at ChangelingPress.com, Amazon, Apple Books, Barnes & Noble, and Kobo/Walmart.

Changeling Press, LLC
ChangelingPress.com

Printed in Great Britain
by Amazon